PRAISE FOR RANDY WAYNE WHITE
AND HIS NOVELS

GRAND CAYMAN SLAM

Randy Wayne White

writing as Randy Striker

A SIGNET BOOK

SIGNET
Published by New American Library, a division of
Penguin Group (USA) Inc., 375 Hudson Street,
New York, New York 10014, USA
Penguin Group (Canada), 90 Eglinton Avenue East, Suite 700, Toronto,
Ontario M4P 2Y3, Canada (a division of Pearson Penguin Canada Inc.)
Penguin Books Ltd., 80 Strand, London WC2R 0RL, England
Penguin Ireland, 25 St. Stephen's Green, Dublin 2,
Ireland (a division of Penguin Books Ltd.)
Penguin Group (Australia), 250 Camberwell Road, Camberwell, Victoria 3124,
Australia (a division of Pearson Australia Group Pty. Ltd.)
Penguin Books India Pvt. Ltd., 11 Community Centre, Panchsheel Park,
New Delhi - 110 017, India
Penguin Group (NZ), 67 Apollo Drive, Rosedale, North Shore 0632,
New Zealand (a division of Pearson New Zealand Ltd.)
Penguin Books (South Africa) (Pty.) Ltd., 24 Sturdee Avenue,
Rosebank, Johannesburg 2196, South Africa

Penguin Books Ltd., Registered Offices:
80 Strand, London WC2R 0RL, England

Published by Signet, an imprint of New American Library,
a division of Penguin Group (USA) Inc.

First Printing, May 1982
First Printing (Author Introduction), April 2009
10 9 8 7 6 5 4 3 2 1

For the Duke . . . and Trav

Introduction

In the winter of 1980, I received a surprising phone call from an editor at Signet Books—surprising because, as a Florida fishing guide, the only time New Yorkers called me was to charter my boat. And if any of my clients were editors, they were savvy enough not to admit it.

The editor said she'd read a story by me in *Outside Magazine* and was impressed. Did I have time to talk?

As a mediocre high school jock, my idols were writers, not ball players. I had a dream job as a light-tackle guide, yet I was still obsessed with my own dream of writing for a living. For years, before and after charters, I'd worked hard at the craft. Selling a story to *Outside,* one of the country's finest publications, was a huge break. I was about to finish a novel, but this was the first time New York had called.

Yes, I had time to talk.

The editor, whose name was Joanie, told me Signet wanted to launch a paperback thriller series that featured a recurring he-man hero. "We want at least four writers on the project because we want to keep the books coming, publishing one right after the other, to create momentum."

Four writers producing books with the same character?

"Characters," Joanie corrected. "Once we get going, the cast will become standard."

Signet already had a template for the hero. He was a Vietnam vet turned Key West fishing guide, she said, talking as if the man existed. He was surfer-boy blond, and he'd been friends with Hemingway.

I am not a literary historian, but all my instincts told me the timetable seemed problematic. I said nothing.

"He has a shark scar," Joanie added, "and he's freakishly strong. Like a man who lifts weights all the time."

The guys I knew who lifted weights were also freakishly clumsy, so . . . maybe the hero, while visiting a local aquarium, tripped during feeding time?

My brain was already problem-solving.

"He lives in Key West," she said, "so, of course, he has to be an expert on the area. That's why I'm calling. You live in Key West, and I liked your magazine story a lot. It seems like a natural fit."

Actually, I fished out of Sanibel Island, on Florida's Gulf Coast, a six-hour drive from Sloppy Joe's, but this was no time for petty details.

"Have you ever been to Key West?" I asked the editor. "Great sunsets."

Editors, I have since learned, can also be cagey. Joanie didn't offer me the job. She had already settled on three of the four writers, she said, but if I was willing to submit a few sample chapters on speculation, she'd give me serious consideration.

Money? A contract? That stuff was "all standard," she told me, and could be discussed later.

"I'll warn you right now," she said, "there are a couple of other writers we're considering, so you need to get at least three chapters to me within a month. Then I'll let you know."

I hung up the phone, stunned by my good fortune. My first son, Lee, had been born only a few months earlier. My much-adored wife, Debra, and I were desperate for money because the weather that winter had been miserable for fishing. But it was *perfect* for writing.

I went to my desk, determined not to let my young family down.

At Tarpon Bay Marina, where I was a guide, my friend Ralph Woodring owned a boat with *Dusky* painted in big blue letters on the side. My friend, Graeme Mellor, lived on a Morgan sailboat named *No Mas*.

Dusky MacMorgan was born.

Every winter, Clyde Beatty-Cole Bros. Circus came to town. Their trapeze artists, I realized, were not only freakishly strong, but they were also freakishly nimble.

Dusky gathered depth.

One of my best friends was the late Dr. Harold Westervelt, a gifted orthopedic surgeon. Dr. Westervelt became the Edison of Death, and he loved introducing himself that way to new patients. His son, David, became Westy O'Davis, and our spear-fishing pal, Billy, became Billy Mack.

Problems with my hero's shark scar and his devoted friendship with Hemingway were also solved.

Working around the clock, pounding away at my old black manual typewriter, I wrote *Key West Connection* in nine days. On a Monday morning, I waited for the post office to open to send it to New York.

Joanie sounded a little dazed when she telephoned on Friday. Was I willing to try a second book on spec?

Hell yes.

God, I was beginning to *love* New York's can-do attitude.

The other three writers (if they ever existed) were fired, and I became the sole proprietor of Captain Dusky MacMorgan—although Signet owned the copyright and all other rights after I signed Joanie's "standard" contract. (This injustice was later made right by a willing and steadfast publisher and my brilliant agent.)

If Joanie (a fine editor) feels badly about that today, she shouldn't. I would've signed for less.

I wrote seven of what I would come to refer to as "duck and fuck" books because in alternating chapters Dusky would duck a few bullets, then spend much-deserved time alone with a heroine.

Seldom did a piece of paper go into my old typewriter that was ripped out and thrown away, and I suspect that's the way the books read. I don't know. I've never reread them. I do remember using obvious clichés, a form of self-loathing, as if to remind myself that I should be doing my *own* writing, not this job-of-work.

The book you are now holding, and the other six, constituted a training arena for a young writer who took seriously the discipline demanded by his craft and also the financial imperatives of being a young father.

For years, I apologized for these books. I no longer do.

—Randy Wayne White
Cartagena, Colombia

I

The corpse was gone, but the sprawled outline was still there—traced in white chalk.

The floor was of pale wood. Not pine. Some kind of tropical planking that held the metallic stink of blood: a black amoeba splotch that had rivered beyond the chalk confines and dried.

"You found her just like this?"

"Aye. I did, mate."

"And they think you murdered her?"

"They *thought* I'd murdered her. Can you imagine? A sweet lad from the home soil like meself!"

I turned away from the outline on the floor. The cop who had traced the corpse had caught the feminine curvature of hips and the delicate fingers of her left hand, which had been thrown out wildly to stop her fall.

Only there was no stopping that fall.

It was the final descent.

Death.

There was something grotesque about a thing so temporary as chalk marking the resting spot of a being who had lived and laughed and loved only to rendezvous, facedown, with wood and a knife slit across her throat.

That plus the stink made me feel unexpectedly queasy. Unexpected because I've seen plenty of death before. But there was a coldness to this white outline of a woman who I would never know. Like so many things the cops do, it seemed to reduce murder to a faceless shape, complete with bloodstain.

"Mind if we step out onto the porch?"

"Aye. I canna stand the sight of the blinkin' thing meself."

I followed him outside. The screen door slammed behind us. Beyond the black growth of gumbo-limbo, mahogany, and jasmine, stars threw paths upon the Caribbean Sea. It was one of those soft winter nights in the tropics. The sort of night people come to Grand Cayman to enjoy. The wind was cloying, blowing off the sea, and you could hear the roar of waves upon the reef, half a mile out.

"You knew her, right?"

The features of my good friend Wes O'Davis

seemed softer by the yellow porch light. Or maybe by the finding of a dead woman upon his living room floor. There was the broad Gaelic face and the Viking beard and the ugly broken nose—but the pale eyes seemed withdrawn, as if he were someplace else.

"Did I know tha' poor wee girl? Aye, I knew her. Treated 'er like a tramp, I did."

"Is this a confession?"

"Hah! Might as well be, lad. Might as well be." He stepped off the porch and kicked at a big conch shell—forgetting he was barefoot, apparently. He jumped around for a second, then grabbed the shell and gave it a savage toss. You could hear it hit the water. "I treated her like a brute, I did," he said.

"But you didn't kill her?"

"N' do I look like a murderer to you, Mr. Dusky MacMorgan?"

"You *look* like you are capable of robbing churches and assaulting nuns."

"I take it that's a yes."

"It is."

"So you think I killed her?"

"I didn't say that. I know you, remember? I know you're no murderer. But you called me down here to help, right? So let me help. Shake off that case of the guilts you have at least long enough to tell me what in hell happened. Ever since I got here you've been tight as a drum. A blacksmith couldn't get a pin up your ass with a hammer. Just relax—I'm a friend, remember?"

He rolled his shoulders, flexing his neck. Then he gave a sudden leprechaun grin that I knew well. "Yer right. I'll be needin' to fill you in on all the particulars—if yer ta help me, that is."

"Okay. Good. So talk. You knew the girl."

"Aye. Monster that I am, I knew her the way I've known a hundred other lonely tourist ladies. They come to Grand Cayman by themselves or with a husband who is no longer very attentive."

"Then you step in."

He nodded. "In me own defense, Yank, I must say most o' them seem the happier for it."

"What was her name?"

"Cynthia. Cynthia Rothchild. Met 'er at one of those snooty little teas in Georgetown. We're still very English here in Caymans, ye know."

"She was wealthy?"

"Said she was a nanny. Had the care of a boy child fer some very rich folks from London. Sir Conan James and Lady James. Sir Conan has an advisory position with Government House, appointed by Her Majesty. That's why I was invited to the snooty tea."

"As a bodyguard?"

He shrugged. " 'Tis probably the real reason.

But they said me attendance was required so they could present me with some damnable award."

I smiled. "From the Queen?"

"Aye. Pretty little thing it is, too. Lady James pinned it on. A great beauty, that Lady James. Magnificent woman—even if she is English."

"But you settled for the nanny, Cynthia Roth-child."

"Aye. She was something of a beauty herself, Yank. Very black hair. Lovely figure. You know me weakness fer the ladies. Saw her three—no, four times. She'd drive her wee rental car over from Three Mile Beach when the lad was asleep."

"And spend the night?"

"Aye. The best part of it."

"So she lived on the island."

"Sir Conan keeps a home here. But they live in London."

"And he didn't mind his nanny's sneaking out?"

"He's a bit of a womanizer himself, I'm afraid. So I'm sure he understood. Besides, Her Majesty honored me with an award, remember? Sir Conan would overlook such a thing with me."

"When's the last time you saw her?"

"In the afternoon, day before yesterday. We had lunch together. She seemed very nervous, Yank. Bothered me, it did. She had the lad with 'er—little Tommy. Fine-looking boy, 'bout four-teen. Something of a genius, to hear Lady James talk. A regular wizard. That night I supped at Betty Bay Point, made the round of the pubs with a few of me island mates, and then went home. She was layin' on the floor of me living room. Part o' her dress was ripped away. She had this awful look o' surprise on 'er face. Her throat had been cut."

"And you called the police?"

"Aye. Rang up the substation at Boddentown. The constable is a friend of mine. He seemed very sorry to have to arrest me. That's when I called you."

"I was kind of surprised you met me at the airport."

"They knew straightaway I didn't do it. I was with me mates, remember. Besides, Sir Conan found the note."

"What note?"

The Irishman picked up another conch shell and threw it in a moonlit spiral toward the sea. "The ransom note, Yank. They've taken little Tommy. Kidnapped 'im, they did. Sir Conan has seventy-two hours to pay them two million pounds. So that gives us three days to find the kidnappers, snatch the lad, and bring him safely home."

"Wait a minute—does Sir Conan want you to get involved?"

"Her Majesty does, Yank. It's a dangerous precedent to set—a true Irishman serving the Queen. But they killed me little Cynthia. And she was a fine sweet girl with a pretty laugh and a wonderful way beneath the covers. She was too good for the likes of me, Yank. Treated 'er like nothin' but a sleepover. So now it's me dooty to make amends. And yer jest mean enough to help. Three days, Yank—that's all we have. An' three days is all those bloody buggers have to live. . . ."

2

It was a coincidence that I happened to be at the marina in Key West when Westy's telephone call for help came in.

I had left my weathered house built on stilts a mile out upon the Calda Bank flats early that morning. Usually when I charter I point my thirty-four-foot sportfisherman toward the Gulf Stream. But on this particular morning, an old and valued client was in town and he had a yearning to pole the flats in search of bonefish and permit.

Sportsmen from the great gray northlands find their taste in fishing changes in direct proportion to the number—and type—of fishing magazines they have read before flying south. And this orthopedic surgeon from Bryan, Ohio, had spent a brutal February and March poring over articles on the flats masters.

So he arrived at the docks at dawn, new fishing cap upon his head and Polaroids strung around his neck on mono line, a dreamy, boyish grin on his face.

It was one of those pink and iridescent blue sunrises unique to the Keys. Along with the diesel smell of the harbor came the jasmine and frangipani spice of Key West on a freshening south wind out of Cuba.

"Damn," was all he could say, his face glazed with pleasure. "Damn, I don't care if the fish hit or not. It's just something being here."

He wasn't lying. He was one of the rare clients: one of the rare sportsmen who hire me because they see fishing as both pleasure and poem. He was among the few I really enjoyed fishing with; a man who did not gauge the success of a trip by the number of iced fish carcasses he could stack on the dock upon our return. So the two of us climbed into my little Boston Whaler and powered off toward the flats of distant Content Key, the little skiff stretching across the clear water as if upon air, brain coral and sea fans appearing and disappearing beneath us as if upon some screen of personal reminiscence.

I had gone over the tide charts carefully beforehand, marking the ascent of tide peaks in my own mind, plotting a fishing itinerary that should guarantee us that epic intersection: a bonefish or permit foraging upon the same flat that held our bait.

It turned out to be a good day. He thought it a great day. He landed and released three good bonefish, then lost a permit to a staghorn after two Homeric runs that made his reel scream as if about to explode.

He had big plans for the next morning. And the next. And I was more than willing. After spending a month alone on my stilthouse listening to my shortwave and eating my own cooking and forcing myself to complete a daily exercise routine that would test a Spartan, I was looking forward to fishing with a friend and eating black beans and yellowtail at the El Cacique and drinking cold beer with my buddies at the dock.

But Westy's call ended all that.

I was out washing down the Whaler when the call came. Steve Wise, America's version of a houseboat David Niven, came ambling barefooted out of the marina office to get me.

"Phone for you."

"This late?"

"And it's not even a lady."

"Didn't give his name?"

"No. But it sounds like he's calling from Mars."

All phone systems are reflections of their own community. New York's is chaotic. Key West's is erratic. The Caribbean phone people really don't seem to give a damn. If it's not too hot, they can fix it tomorrow.

Westy did, indeed, sound as if he were calling from Mars.

"Yank! It's meself, Wes O'Davis!"

"I can barely hear you."

"Aye—because yer gettin' old an' fat and yer ears are dyin'."

"And you are spending a lot of money on this call, old friend, so I assume it's important—so what's new?"

"Other than bein' jailed for murder, not much."

"Did you say murder?"

"Hah—see, yer ears are givin' out!"

So I lined up another guide for my fishing friend from Ohio, called the airline and made reservations for a flight from Key West to Miami and from Miami to Caymans, then climbed back in the Whaler and burrowed through the spring darkness across five miles of tricky water to my stilthouse.

One thing about living alone—there's never any trouble packing.

I stuffed shorts and a half-dozen shirts, running shoes, and razor blades into a canvas satchel. I thought for a moment, then added my lucky Limey knickers, black watch sweater, and cap—and finally the cold weight of my Randall attack/survival knife.

You can bet that when O'Davis is around, trouble can't be far behind.

So in the spring heat of a dank Miami afternoon I climbed aboard a DC-10 that seemed somehow safer for its experience, then settled back in my narrow seat in second class. First class gives you a tad more room—which you can use when you're my size—but it also suggests the sort of monetary hoity-toity crap that I hate.

So I settled back while the big engines smoked and wheezed and watched the white concrete mass of Miami drop away and fade as we climbed to twenty thousand, where yachts were toy-sized amid the blue depths and green shallows of the great Atlantic.

There was a holiday atmosphere aboard the plane. And why not? Grand Cayman has rapidly become the Caribbean's tourist hot spot. There's great diving, fine fishing, and plenty of long white beaches. The three islands—Grand Cayman, Cayman Brac, and Little Cayman—were relatively unknown to the American tourist trade until the early 1960s because they are so remote: 150 miles south of Cuba and far off the Bahama chain.

So Americans were content to bake themselves and spend their dollars in the more accessible Bahamas until the Bahamians got greedy, then turned surly, and finally became downright dangerous to any American foolish enough to want to vacation there.

Then word about the Caymans began to leak out. The islanders—a handsome mixed race of French, Spanish, Scottish, and African—were friendly and the rates were ridiculously inexpensive.

The islanders are still friendly—probably because they've always been treated as equals by their British sovereigns.

But it's no longer inexpensive.

Even so, the manifest of pale Northerners who flew with me seemed hellbent on making the most of this Caribbean vacation. While the flight attendants passed out complimentary rum punches, newlyweds made moon eyes and dive enthusiasts leafed through the scuba cult magazines and newly retired factory workers blinked at the expanse and light of open sea like kids seeing the world for the first time.

I traded in my rum punch for cold beer and watched the western tip of Cuba roll by in fields of sugarcane and pasture beneath us. Castro leases us two air routes over his little Commie paradise: one to the east, the other over the western tip. This route wasn't that far from Havana—and closer yet to Mariel Harbor. During Carter's refugee boatlift debacle, I had spent a long and dangerous evening there. It didn't exactly bring back pleasant memories. But my mission there had produced some valuable friendships. Sipping at my beer, I thought about the beautiful Androsa Santarun, who had been sired by a father she could never acknowledge. I wondered if I would ever see her again.

And I thought about Wes O'Davis, too. I had met him in Mariel. And he had saved my life. Not once, but twice.

So when he called for help, there was no indecision on my part. His was a debt I could never truly repay.

So I was thinking about all these things when I noticed that the flight attendant who had brought my beer was staring at me. They don't like to be called "stewardess" anymore. And I can't blame them. People in any profession should have the right to be called what they damn well please.

She had long smoky brown hair and a mahogany complexion that suggested Caribbean antecedents. Her airline uniform was a calf-length dress and a suitcoat over a white blouse. The suitcoat dutifully tried to cover the heavy swell of mammary development—but failed. An impossible job on this woman. She had quizzical brown eyes that snapped away when she saw me returning her look. I guessed her to be about twenty-two or twenty-three. She wore no makeup and little jewelry. Few women can let themselves go into public without even the barest of beauty props—but this lady was obviously one of the few. She didn't need them. She had a delicate, expressive face and a complexion that suggested a childhood spent on a tropical island where everyone bathed in coconut milk.

I felt her eyes lock on me twice more as the DC-10 roared through the thin air of twenty thousand feet, over beautiful Isle of Pines and the other small islands of southern Cuba.

I have been lucky enough with women—but I'm nowhere near in that film-star category of men which makes beautiful women press motel keys into their hands. I am big enough, but my hair is sun-bleached and matted, and I have scars enough on face and hands to frighten the weak of heart.

And this was one very beautiful woman.

So it was a mystery. I toyed with it for a while, then decided to find out just what in the hell her interest was. No easy task, really. Flight attendants have seen every conceivable brand of come-on. Especially the pretty ones.

Finally, I finished my beer and signaled for another. She smiled as she walked down the narrow aisle.

"Something else to drink?"

"Another bottle of this, if you have it."

"We have plenty. Everyone else is drinking the rum punch."

"Great. I hope they drink it all."

"It really isn't bad. You should try it."

"Is that why you've been staring at me? Wondering why I won't drink your punch?"

She stiffened for a moment. "I wasn't staring at you." And then she laughed. "Well, I guess maybe I was."

"I thought maybe I had something caught between my teeth. It worried me."

"Oh, your teeth are fine. It's just that I thought I recognized you."

"Shouldn't I be saying that?"

"Lord, I guess that does sound like some awful line."

"Not so awful, because I have a feeling you mean it."

"Oh, I do. I used to work for another airline and we carried a lot of the pro teams. I keep thinking that I've seen you before. And the only place I can think we might have met is maybe on some flight. Are you a professional baseball player or something like that?"

"Baseball has never gotten desperate enough to sign someone who hits the curve as poorly as I do."

"Football? You look like a football player."

I shook my head, smiling. Closer, she was even prettier. Silent, she was the picture of composure. But when she spoke, with her soft Cayman accent, she had just the slightest syncopation of speech that suggested she might have stuttered as a child. "I'm way too clumsy to be a football player," I said.

She eyed me carefully. "I'm not sure I believe that. You look anything but clumsy to me." An electronic bell chimed softly behind her. It was the signal to prepare for landing. She grinned at me and gave a shrug. "Maybe we met in another life then, huh?"

"If we did, I was a fool to leave it."

"How nice of you to say." She hesitated for a moment, torn between conversation and her job. "Will you be staying on Grand Cayman long?" she asked quickly.

"I'm not sure. I've got some business to take care of. I suppose you'll be flying out tonight."

"No—I've got a week off. Some other girls

and I keep an apartment there. It's better than staying with my parents. I'm just going to lie around the pool . . ."

"And drink punch?"

"It really is good. I think you ought to stop by and have some."

"Maybe I will."

"Diacona Ebanks." She held out a soft hand, and I held it briefly. "My friends call me Dia."

"And my name is MacMorgan. Dusky."

She smiled again. "I'm at the Sea Mist Apartments, Mr. MacMorgan. Make sure you stop by. I feel I owe you something for being so rude. People shouldn't stare, you know."

With that, she moved away, slim hips and smoke-brown hair swaying, bracing herself against airpockets as we readied ourselves for descent.

I felt the stares of passengers seated nearby on the back of my head, and I saw the looks of envy from the vacationing men. She was some pretty lady, and I couldn't blame them.

Below, the sea was a turquoise desert glazed with copper. The sun was wheeling westward, low on the horizon, setting toward another day, other countries, and other lives.

The plane banked to port, bringing Grand Cayman into view. The island looked gem-like, lush and vulnerable on the immensity of sea. Georgetown was a modern cluster of white

buildings fronted by a harbor where old wind
ships rested at anchor. A few lights were blink-
ing on inland, and the arrowing strip of runway
was illuminated as if craft from outer space
were expected.

People jumped to their feet and grabbed their
baggage the moment the plane came to a stop. I
sat comfortably, sipping at my beer. Why people
force themselves to stand in line when they
don't have to is beyond me. Dia Ebanks slipped
me a smile. I was the last to disembark.

"Sea Mist Apartments," she reminded me as
I ducked beneath the cabin door. "Right off
Seven Mile Beach."

I took the proffered hand, returned the squeeze,
and said good-bye.

Outside, the clamminess of Miami was replaced by the freshness of an island in the trade
winds. Black policemen in white jackets and
white English helmets nodded and smiled.
Owen Roberts was a small Caribbean airport,
neater than most. It smelled of asphalt and the
ozone freshness of open sea.

When I had taken her hand, Dia had slipped
me a note. I waited until I had taken care of the
immigration formalities to read it. Westy had
spotted me by then, and he came charging
through the crowd, his big ugly Irish face lit in
a grin.

The note said: "Maybe dinner tonight at ten?"

I turned to look for her somewhere in the confines of the small terminal.

I got just the briefest profile of face, body, and wisp of hair as she disappeared out the door and into the Cayman darkness.

3

"So what do ya say, Yank? Are ya with me?"

The voice of O'Davis jerked me out of my reverie. The sound of sea was wild upon the night reef, and a freshening breeze brought the delicate flower and citrus smell of the island to our place on the porch of the small cottage.

I checked the green glow of my Rolex Submariner. It was almost nine. I'd have to hustle if I wanted to get cleaned up and meet Dia for dinner.

"What you're telling me is that you've been given the assignment by your government to crack these kidnappers before they kill the boy."

"Aye. It's true I've handled tougher cases on me own—but I'd admire havin' yer company, Yank." He winked at me.

"It sounds more like police business than British Secret Service business."

"On an island small as this, mate, everything is everyone else's business." A coldness came into his eyes as he added, "Besides, the girl had become me lover, remember? You told me once, Dusky, that you knew what it was like to lose a lady. Never asked you about it because I had lost a lady meself. I knew how painful the talking of it was. So now I've lost another lady. I didna love her, it's true. But we had been beneath the covers together, and no human ever seems more alive to another than in circumstances such as that. And now she's no more. They didna kill her in a very pretty fashion. And they tried to make it look as if I'd done it."

"In other words, you asked for the assignment."

The coldness was still in his eyes. "Aye, Yank. That I did."

"Then I'm with you a hundred percent."

He smiled and shook his head, rubbing his hands together like someone anxious for supper. "Then it's settled. Tomorrow mornin' we start."

"You have any leads?"

"Nary a one."

"So we meet with Sir Conan and talk to him, right?"

"Aye. We've got to have a look at the note. The island force is checking with immigration to see if someone is new to the island who might be a suspect.''

"When they went over your cottage, did they come up with any fingerprints, anything that might be a clue?"

"Clean as a whistle. They killed her where she fell—that's fer sure. I figure someone followed 'er to me cottage. I never lock the place, so she jest went on in. You could see where she had made herself a drink, waitin' for me. She had put the drink down on the coffee table beside a book. Then she went to the door and died.''

"It seems strange someone would kill her like that. It doesn't make any sense. The boy was back on the west end of the island, right? Back in his parents' house?''

O'Davis shrugged. "Far as anyone knows. That's where they found the note. The lad's bed had been slept in. There were marks of a ladder against the wall and the window was open.''

"So why follow Cynthia Rothchild out here just to kill her? Unless—''

"I know, Yank,'' O'Davis interrupted. "Unless she was involved. Or unless she knew who the kidnappers were. I thought about that meself. In her own way, she was a troubled girl. Beneath the surface, you could see it. I figured she would tell me in time. It crossed me mind that she might be comin' to me fer help."

"On our ride from the airport, we passed a police station in Georgetown and another in Boddentown. If she had seen the kidnappers, why wouldn't she stop at one of those two police stations? Or just wake up Sir Conan James, for that matter."

"Sir Conan wasn't home, for one thing. But yer right, Yank—she'd have stopped at the constable's. She didn't know I served the government in an official capacity."

"What about neighbors?" I asked. "You live on a pretty deserted stretch of road here, but I noticed another cottage down the beach a bit. Maybe they heard something."

"Aye. Me neighbor is crazy old Hubbard Mac-Donnel. A black MacDonnel he is, and a wonderful character. Makes 'is livin' with a few mango trees and by buildin' cottages in the back-time way, usin' ironwood and wattle. Makes his plaster in an old lime kiln."

"Did the police talk to him?"

"They did. But you couldn't expect old Hubbard to tell the officials much. I figure we can catch up with him in the mornin', or tomorrow night on the west end in Hell."

"Hell? Is that a joke?"

He chuckled. "Ye might think so. But it's not.

We got a little settlement on the island the back-timers named Hell because the rock formations there resemble somethin' ye might expect to find down under. Hubbard visits his island mates there at a club called the Inferno."

"Sounds interesting."

"Aye, 'tis."

O'Davis rolled his neck, trying to relax. He went inside and returned with two bottles of Red Stripe beer. He handed me mine, then half-drained his in a gulp.

I reached over and put my hand on his thick shoulder. "Don't worry, Westy. If there's any way to track those guys down in seventy-two hours, well find it."

"Aye, that we will. But the rough part will be separatin' them from the boy."

"One step at a time, O'Davis. We have to figure out who they are, first. And maybe we have a little more to go on than you figured."

"How's that?"

"We have to assume the murder of Cynthia Rothchild and the kidnapping of the kid . . . what's his name?"

"Thomas. Thomas James."

"We have to assume the two are related. They took little Thomas from his bedroom by ladder—it means they had some knowledge of the layout of the house. And they also knew the windows would not be locked. If they'd been unsure about the windows, they wouldn't have even bothered with the ladder. They'd have just picked the lock on the door."

"Aye. I kin see that."

"And we know something else, too."

"What's that?"

"Whoever killed Cynthia knew you weren't home."

"How do you figure, Yank?"

"If they'd known, they'd have murdered her before she went into your house. I think setting you up was an afterthought on their part. And not a very smart one. It was a half-assed job. They obviously didn't know if you would or would not have an alibi. It tells us something about the people involved in this. It tells us they can be hasty. And sloppy. It tells us they take chances. Stupid chances. It means that if we can find them, we can beat them."

O'Davis let his face contort into a soft Irish grin. "Aye. I knew that already, lad. Almost feel sorry for the bloody buggers, I do. Almost."

I had stashed my canvas duffel on the porch of O'Davis' cottage. It was a pretty little three-room cottage of white board and batten built beneath coconut palms on a sandy expanse of beach twenty yards from the edge of the sea. It was fronted by the main road that twisted along

the southern boundary of Grand Cayman between West Bay and East End. Every now and
then a car would go roaring by in the March
night, but mostly there was only the sound of
the wind and sea and the buzz of nocturnal
insects.

The house was built to be open to the sea,
and through the big front window I could look
inside and see the grim outline of the dead
woman on the floor.

O'Davis seemed to read my thoughts. "Not a
very pleasant thing to sleep with."

"I'll get a scrub brush and some heavy cleaner
in town tonight. It'll be gone in the morning."

"I'd appreciate that, Yank. Yer a kind one, ya
are. Couldn't bear the thought o' touchin' the
thing. . . ."

So I showered and shaved in the narrow confines of the cottage bathroom, changed into
clean soft gray pants and a blue cotton shirt.
The trade wind blowing off the sea dried me
more thoroughly than the towel. When I went
outside to ask if I could borrow the Irishman's
car, he was gone. There was only a note on
the table.

Yank—
Here are the keys to the Fiat. Expect you'll be

wantin' to go into town for a beer or two.
Sorry, but I'm just not in the mood. Watch the
brakes—they only work when they want to. We
drive in the proper way on Grand Cayman—
on the left side of the road—but I'm afraid all
the drivers here are as careless as Baptists with-
out a sin to their names. Be careful.

Wes

I took the pen and added "See you tonight or
in the morning" at the bottom of the note, then
went outside to the car.

I had seen O'Davis in his black Irish moods
before, and knew there was nothing to be
gained by trying to console him. I could picture
him outside on the long empty edge of sea with
a bottle of Shannon whiskey held ready in one
big fist while he walked and studied the chaotic
swirl of stars and universe with accusing eyes.

He had said he hadn't loved Cynthia Rothchild. But he had felt something for her. That
was becoming increasingly clear.

And I didn't envy the people who had murdered her once O'Davis caught up with them. I
didn't envy them one bit.

It was a boxy little Fiat with mush for brakes
and a bad muffler. I backed out of the drive
and headed west toward Georgetown. The Fiat
began to miss badly at fifty, and the muffler

made it scream as if I were doing ninety. I rolled down the windows; the rush of wind was cloying with salt and fragrant night.

Through the lasering headlights, island and sea swept past as I headed for Georgetown and my date with this new stranger, Diacona Ebanks. I wondered about this mystery lady as I drove. It's not uncommon for a stewardess to hunt company in a strange town. But Dia was very obviously an islander by birth. So why had she come on to me?

It was a pleasant mystery; something to toy with while I drove. I tried to reconstruct her face in my mind and found I could not. I had not seen her long enough to remember the details of her face. There was only the impression of clear nut-colored skin, big brown eyes, Polynesian hair, and the heavy thrust of breasts beneath flight attendant's jacket.

Jungled growth of mangrove and vines and Cuban laurel pressed in on the twisting road. Calcareous rock protruded from the vines and huge gray land crabs skittered sideways with malevolent eyes.

I drove past Frank's Sound and through the little scattering of houses called Breakers, where the good smell of fried turtle came from the seaside fortress of the Island Club.

It was a pleasant night to drive: bright moon

over the Caribbean; small houses alight, and the
vision of dark island faces passing before windows. A stranger to this isle of pirates, fishermen, green-turtle hunters and English gentry,
I found the atmosphere of a land so dependent
on the sea a palpable thing; an atmosphere easily seen and more easily felt.

I was just passing the island drive-in—a bleak
structure of white and blue with a stark concrete-
block screen—when I noticed the other car in my
rearview mirror.

It came charging around the curve as we
headed into Boddentown, pulled right up on my
bumper, then refused to pass as I slowed and
waved him around.

So close on my bumper was he that I could
see it was some kind of slinky racing machine:
Jaguar or Triumph.

He had bright lights on along with a bank of
fog lamps that blinded me every time I stared
into the mirror.

O'Davis had warned me about the crazy drivers in Grand Cayman—but I didn't think anybody could be that stupid.

I slowed for Boddentown, with its row of
small tin-roofed houses, then pulled off into the
shell drive of the Sand Castle Apartments.

The driver downshifted, tires squealing, then

raced on ahead, disappearing around the curve and down the hill toward Georgetown.

But not for long.

It was a Jag, low-slung and silver. I saw it sitting, lights out, on a dirt road like a cop in a speed trap. Had I seen it soon enough, I would have pulled over and let the driver know just what I thought of his brand of high-speed stupidity.

Instead, I saw him too late and went puttering on by at a stately forty-five miles an hour.

The Jag screamed out behind me, lights on high beam, and began his bumper-to-bumper game again.

And that's when I knew this was no ordinary automotive maniac. Somebody in that car wanted me. And it wasn't long before I knew how badly he wanted me.

It was a desolate stretch of highway between Boddentown and Savanah, with plenty of curves. Every time I slowed for one of the curves, he would come screaming up behind me, touch bumpers, then drop quickly back in case I jammed on the brakes.

There was no danger of that, because the brakes of the Fiat were so bad. He wanted me to stop; wanted me to pull over. That was obvious. And nobody would want that unless he was armed. Well armed.

I changed tactics. I floored the Fiat, little engine screaming as I slid my way through a series of tricky S-curves.

The Jag had no trouble staying right on my tail. The Fiat just wasn't a match. And truthfully, I'm not much of a driver. I hate cars. I'd rather spend ten days on a boat than ten minutes in one of those pot-metal deathtraps. I admit that I like to drive slowly. My friends are all too willing to point out that I drive like an old lady.

The driver of the Jag had no such phobia. Twice he almost nosed me off curves into the jungled mainland. I kept trying to brake unexpectedly so that I could pull in behind him. But the Fiat's brakes just weren't up to it. I had just about decided to stop and make a fight of it when I noticed a turnoff ahead. The sign said it was the road to Newland.

There wasn't much hope of losing the Jag with a sudden turn, but I had to give it a try.

Every time he had tried to nose me off the road, I had clamped on the brakes. And he had come to expect just that—or so I hoped.

At the turnoff, I swung suddenly right. Again he pulled ahead, trying to force me into the ditch. He expected me to brake. But I didn't. Instead, I accelerated, catching his fender with mine. The Jag swerved, then spun on the loose gravel. My Fiat slid dangerously toward the chunks of rock at the edge of the road. I turned the wheel in a wild, uncontrolled drift. I got the car stopped, realizing for the first time my Fiat had stalled. The Jag was about forty yards away. A door swung open as I tried to get my wheezy old engine to start again.

A small slim figure got out, and I saw the revolver gleam before I heard it.

Glass exploded around me. Three times he shot. I crouched down behind the wheel, trying to get the door of the passenger side open before my assassin came to inspect his kill.

I hoped to jump him as he peered into the car. But I never got the chance.

He seemed satisfied with the three shots; inexplicably, he jumped back in the Jag and roared off.

I sat in the new silence, breathing deeply. The Fiat had overheated. The engine tick-tick-ticked, as if affronted by the strain I had put it under.

Land crabs rustled in the bushes, and somewhere a dog barked in the Cayman night.

When I judged it safe, I started the car and headed on in to Georgetown and my dinner date with Dia Ebanks.

4

Her apartment was a concrete-and-stucco multistory structure which, like most of the other buildings on Cayman's Seven Mile Beach, could have just as easily been a part of Miami.

Red and yellow decorator lights were aimed at a trio of coconut palms in front—a particularly nauseating landscaper's trick that only cheapened the place.

While traffic on the east end of the island was sparse to nonexistent, the tourist mecca of Seven Mile Beach was alight with neon and headlights. Newlyweds walked hand in hand and vacationing Americans roamed the streets in flowered shirts, looking in shop windows.

My confrontation with the Jag had made me a little late. I parked the Fiat in a visitor space as the sign ordered, then made my way up the stairs to the second floor. Her apartment was 23A. The door was made of steel with a little glass peephole. The hole darkened momentarily after I rang and then the door swung open.

I watched her face closely.

"Dusky!"

No trace of surprise in her voice—just a cordial delight in seeing her guest had arrived.

"Sorry I'm late, Dia. Had some car trouble."

She led me across plush carpet, past modern bamboo and cast-iron furniture, saying as she went, "Now that you're in the Caymans you mustn't worry about always being on time." She laughed pleasantly. "Believe me, no one else here does."

The apartment had a veranda that looked out onto the harbor. Boats at anchor were lighted in the glaze of moon, and voices trickled across the water like wind chimes. I took a seat on one of the porch chairs that faced the water.

"Would you like something to drink? I bought Red Stripe beer just for you."

"That would be fine."

She handed me the cold bottle and poured a glass of white wine for herself.

There was that awkward pause of strangers in potentially intimate circumstances before she took a seat.

"Nice night."

"Beautiful. I love the moon on the water. That's why we chose this apartment."

"You and another flight attendant?"

"Myself and two others. But we're hardly ever here at the same time. It works out perfectly." She hesitated. "There are two bedrooms—but only one double bed. And I hate small beds. Don't you?"

She wore one of those terry-cloth running suits made by New York designers for people who never run. Short shorts and tennis shirt were both white with burnt-orange trim. It made her skin look three shades darker than it really was and added a coconut-oil gloss to her hair. The fingernails of the hand which held her wineglass were long and carefully manicured. She wore a few pieces of dainty jewelry: a slim gold chain around an ankle, a ring with birthstone, two folds of intricate necklace that draped toward the veeing of her terry-cloth shirt and the heavy thrust of breasts. When the light was just right, through the white material, you could see that she was quite braless. Her face was a beautiful composite of Cayman's four hundred years of seafaring infidelities: Indian, Negro, Spanish, and Scotch—it was all there in the perfect curvature of cheeks and nose and delicate jaw. Her eyes were so dark that they seemed to suggest mystery, and when they caught mine, they seemed to glow.

With all of this was something else; something nurtured by Dia Ebanks on her own. It was a surprising air of sophistication, an air of the cosmopolitan probably developed through her profession.

Superficially, she seemed at ease. It was as if having a big blond stranger in her apartment was nothing out of the ordinary. But beneath that, I could see something else: a furtive nervousness that I couldn't decipher. I couldn't tell if she was uneasy because of me—or something else.

In her soft Cayman accent, Dia Ebanks asked, "You said earlier that you came to the islands on business, Dusky. Do you mind if I ask what your business is?"

"Not at all. I run charterboats in Key West. I came to Grand Cayman at the request of a friend to see about setting up a similar business."

"Another charter boat service on this island?" She chuckled softly. "Heavens, I can't imagine there's any need. Every man and boy I know charters."

"What, no woman captains?"

She cocked her head ever so slightly. Her long raven hair cascaded over her shoulder. "I

thought about it. No—don't laugh! I did. My
father was a sailing captain, and my grand-
father, and his father before him. All wind
captains. They would hunt the green turtle.
Sometimes they would take me with them on
short trips when I was a little girl. It was all
so . . . fine. The men and their jokes, and the
smell of the boat and seeing the big green turtles
pulled up in the traps. I loved it. I did. I wanted
to be a boy for the longest time."

"I'm probably one of many who are very glad
you didn't get your wish."

She laughed. "That's kind of you to say—but
I was horribly disappointed for a time. But then,
when I was fifteen or sixteen, I began to . . .
develop. There was no doubt I was going to be
female. A New York fashion model was on the
island shooting a display for a big magazine. He
saw me, asked me to pose, and suddenly I was
making more money than my poor parents."

"You went to New York?"

"Yes. For one horrible year. When I was eigh-
teen. It was an education. I learned to appreciate
the finer things in life, though. But that exposure
made it . . . well, impossible to return to Cayman and live full time. Like that wonderful
book *You Can't Go Home Again*. It's true. The
people here hadn't changed. But I had."

"Why didn't you continue your modeling?"

She smirked. "I wanted to. But they didn't want me by the time I was twenty. How many . . . full-figured girls do you see modeling clothes? And by the time I was twenty I was becoming a little overdeveloped. So I decided being a flight attendant would be the perfect job for me. I could still live in the Caymans, but I could also live away from them. It's like living two lives."

"And you're satisfied?"

She thought for a moment. "Sometimes I'm sorry I ever left the island. Sometimes I wish I had just married one of the local fishermen and settled down with about a dozen kids and a couple of turtle traps. I feel that way when my life begins to seem a little too complicated. Like now . . ."

"Now?"

I saw the old nervousness return to her eyes. The moon was high over the apartment balcony, and her face was lovely and easy to read. She suddenly looked at her watch. "I like you, Dusky."

"Great," I said. "Does that mean you're about to tell me something, Dia?"

She nodded. "When I saw you on the plane, I pictured you as another type of man. The self-important athlete type; big and brash and not easily hurt. But I was wrong. You're quiet and understanding, and your eyes tell me you care for people. . . ."

"Dia, just what in the hell are you getting at?"

Suddenly, there was a loud pounding at the door. "Oh Lord," Dia said, "he's here already." She got to her feet quickly, wringing her hands.

"Dia, do you mind telling me—"

"Dusky! I've got to hide you."

"What?"

"Really. I don't normally just invite strange men to my apartment. Can't you see—I was using you. Just trust me for a moment and hide."

I grabbed her by the wrist and swung her around so that she faced me. The pounding on the door was getting more insistent now. "Dia, I'm not the hiding type. And dammit, unless you tell me exactly what's going on, I'm going to answer the door myself."

"No!"

"Then tell me. And make it quick."

She took a deep breath. I held her hands in mine. She was shaking.

"Okay," she said, "but then you have to hide."

"Let's hear it."

She lowered her voice to a whisper. "Six months ago I became involved with a very important man on the island. A married man. I knew it was wrong, but for a time it didn't matter. I loved him and I thought he loved me. But he didn't. Later I found out that he was involved with several other women at the same time. For the last two weeks I've been trying to end it. I even had my locks changed. I knew that he would come to me tonight after his wife was asleep. He always does. So I just decided to make sure I had company when he arrived. He has a terrible temper, so I had to make sure it was a man big enough to defend himself. I know it was an awful thing to do . . ."

"That's right."

"And I'm sorry, Dusky. I really am."

I dropped her hands and went toward the door. She ran and jumped in front of me, knocking her wineglass over in the process.

She was almost begging now. "Please," she said. "Please, just hide in the closet for a few minutes and let me answer the door."

"Why the hell should I? Neither of us is doing anything wrong."

She sniffed and brushed at her hair, gathering her composure. "If he's not gone five minutes after I open the door, you can come out. I was wrong. I know that now. But I was also very frightened. Just this once, Dusky, do what I say. I know we really don't know each other. But I can see there's understanding in you, and you have to believe that I am normally not like this. It would mean so much to me."

So I followed the old vaudeville routine, the one where the secret lover hides from the murderous husband. The fact that I was no secret lover and he was not her husband made it all the more ludicrous. I got down on hands and knees and crawled into the dark hall closet, hiding myself as best I could behind a rack of dresses. The closet smelled of lavender, and I kept wishing Oliver Hardy was there so he could turn, nod his head and say, "Here's another fine mess you've gotten me into!"

I kept the door cracked so I could see into the living room. Diacona Ebanks hustled around the apartment, hiding my beer and straightening the cushions.

"Be there in a minute," she yelled.

The man continued to pound on the door.

There was a mirror in the hall through which I got a partial view of the bathroom. She didn't shut the door behind her. I watched her strip shorts and shirt off, got a fleeting glimpse of the large and perfect upturned breasts before she pulled on an old bathrobe and wrapped a towel around her head. As a final touch, she smeared some kind of green complexion gook all over her face.

"I'm coming," she yelled, hurrying toward the door.

Her anxious lover was a tall man with conservative black hair. He wore a white dinner jacket and dark slacks. He was a lot older than Diacona, maybe forty-five. He had ruddy good looks and a refined manner.

Dia opened the door, blocking his entrance.

"What in the bloody hell took you so long?" His accent was British.

"Jimmy, can't you see? I was in the bathroom."

"Bathroom . . . humph. So I see. What, may I ask, is that mess on your face?"

Dia still stood in the doorway, refusing to let him enter. "Jimmy, I told you it was over. Please believe me. I'm still fond of you, but it's an impossible situation and I don't want to see you again."

He had the cruel smile I had seen before on a certain type of English army officer. "Yes," he said, "and you didn't want to see me last week or the week before that or the week before that. But you always do, Dia. And you always will. You may loathe me in the bright light of day, but you can't get enough of me in a dark bedroom—isn't that right, Dia?"

For a moment she seemed on the edge of hysteria, as if she were about to launch herself toward his face. But she visibly gathered herself, voice still calm. "You couldn't be more wrong, Jimmy. You must believe that. And I warn you—if you ever come to my home again I'll have no choice but to call the authorities. Or your wife."

And suddenly, his pomp and inflated ego fizzled like a worn balloon. He remained just long enough to save face, trying to shatter Dia's composure with ugly words. But she let him have his say, then shut and locked the door when he was gone.

I got to my feet, banged my head on a shelf, and stepped out into the hall.

"You handled that pretty well," I said.

She took a step toward me, opened her mouth as if to speak, then her face collapsed into one long uncontrollable sob. She hesitated when I opened my arms to her, then fell upon my chest crying.

"How . . . how . . . how could he speak to me that way? After all . . . all our times together. . . ."

Her words fell apart as she sobbed.

So what do you do when a strange lady chooses your shoulder to cry upon? There's not much you can do. You stroke the soft hair and pat the back and make comforting sounds, feeling like a fool all the while because there's no way in hell you can help.

You can just be there.

She cried so long and hard that she began to hiccup, and that made her laugh, then cry some more and finally laugh again.

"My God, I must look a mess," she groaned in her soft Cayman accent. "I've gotten this"—*hiccup*—"face cream all over your nice blue shirt, and I made you hide in a closet. Dusky, you must"—*hiccup*—"rue the moment you accepted my invitation."

"No I don't. I've had more excitement tonight than I've had in a long time."

"Well, I insist that you at least stay for dinner after all . . . this. A good meal is the least I can do."

"What I really think, Dia, is that you ought to grab a shower, have another glass of wine, and go to bed. I'll call you in the morning if you want."

She looked up at me with those big dark eyes, the goo on her face unable to hide the beauty of her. "Please, Dusky," she whispered. "Please. I don't want to be alone for a while. Stay. Just for a bit, okay?"

"Okay. On one condition."

"Anything."

"Wash that green stuff off your face. Or I'll feel as if I'm having dinner with an acne commercial."

"God, I must look awful!"

She rushed off to the bathroom while I got another beer from the refrigerator. I took my time with the cold Red Stripe and toured the apartment. It was a woman's place, no doubt about that. It had all the required knickknacks: butterflies mounted in a glass box, plaster of Paris gnomes and elves on tables, silk flowers in woven baskets, and a stack of *Cosmopolitan* magazines beneath the coffee table. Everything was in its place, neat and clean and sterile. I have been seeing more and more apartments and homes like this one inhabited by the three flight attendants. There is a prepackaged atmosphere about such places. The decorations don't matter because no one stays there long enough to add a touch of personality. It may well be the mandate of our own transitory lives: Everyone should have at least three home bases, because, after all, isn't mobility what the future is all about? Don't worry about the *quality* of the life you live. Worry about the *quantity*. Such places suggest—and wrongly—that mobility is synonymous with experience. And why not gobble up all the experience you can in a lifetime? The result is that the apartments and homes of the world's transients take on the bleak glow of bus terminals.

I suddenly understood Diacona's wistful ex-

pression when she mentioned that she sometimes regretted not marrying one of the local
fishermen and remaining a permanent fixture on
the island.

A hundred, or even forty, years ago, she
would have. And she would have probably gone
on to live a pretty reasonable life. But now she
found herself trapped in certain ways by her
own worldliness.

Just as we all do.

She reappeared from the bathroom wearing
the same white jogging outfit, but looking fresher
and happier than before.

"You found the beer? Good."

"And you look very pretty indeed, Miss Diacona Ebanks."

"Thank you. You don't know how much I appreciate your staying, Dusky. Just having someone to talk to will make me feel a lot better."

"And some food would make me feel better
yet."

I helped her cook. She broiled wahoo steaks
she had picked up on the way from the airport.
I added lime and garlic and butter. She kept
handing me beer and refilling her wineglass.
More than once she said that she was a light
drinker but tonight she felt like she needed it.

I didn't argue.

So we ate the good fish and salad and hot turtle

chowder on the veranda overlooking Georgetown harbor. It was one of those common tropical nights that always seem too rare: moon-glazed sea, wind in the palms, the lights of boats blending with the glimmer of stars on the dark horizon.

When we had finished, I helped her with the dishes. I washed. She dried. I had more beer. She had more wine. There was something I wanted to ask her before she got too tipsy. The right time never really came. I kept expecting her to mention her sophisticated boyfriend, Jimmy. But she never did.

Finally, I had to take the lead.

"He didn't seem like that bad a guy, really."

"Jimmy? Oh."

I waited through the silence, then went on, "Was there any way he could have known that I was coming to visit you tonight?"

She looked at me, a new sharpness in her eyes. "Why? Are you frightened?"

"Scared to death. It's just that I had an interesting drive into Georgetown. Someone in a silver Jaguar tried to run me off the road, then took a few wild shots at me."

For a second, I thought she was going to drop her glass. "Is this a joke? Are you kidding?"

"Does your Jimmy drive a silver Jag?"

"No. A Mercedes. And he's not my Jimmy.

My God, why didn't you go to the police? You might have been killed!"

I smiled at her. "Well, I was late for our date as it was. And I was hungry."

She fixed her eyes on me for a long time. Then she returned my smile. "You are something, Dusky MacMorgan."

"And you are getting drunk, Miss Diacona Ebanks."

"I'm not!"

"Hah! The first symptom of alcoholism—you won't admit that you're drunk."

She flipped the dish towel at me. I caught it and gave a tug. She could have resisted. But she didn't. She came tumbling, laughing into my arms. We half wrestled, half nuzzled for a time. Then she turned her face up to mine. The kitchen was well lit with neon. There were gold flecks at the edge of her dark eyes. She had a small crescent scar above her eyebrow, probably from some childhood accident. Her lips were dark and full, lightly glazed with some kind of lipstick.

"Sir, I hardly even know you," she said vampishly.

"That's right," I said. "That's right."

She lifted her face up to mine, touching my lips with her nose, her cheek, tracing zeros upon the small of my back with her fingernail.

I kissed her softly, then pulled away, not wanting to hurry her. But she grabbed a small fistful of hair and forced my face back down to her open mouth, her tongue hot and alive and searching.

"Please," she said. "Don't leave me tonight."

"You're very convincing."

"You make me want to be convincing."

I traced the edge of her chin with my mouth while my hands separated shirttail from jogging shorts, then slid up the warm ribbed curvature of her.

She moaned softly, eyes closed, head thrown back.

"The fashion photographer was right. You have developed beyond your years."

"Ah . . . isn't it . . . awful?"

"Awesome might be more to the . . . point."

"Is that a pun?"

"I don't know. Let's see."

Kissing her, I bent and lifted her off the floor and carried her through the living room to the veranda. There was a wide deck recliner there. She stood, watched me for a moment with a strange smile, then pulled the terry-cloth shirt over her head in one sure motion.

"What do you think?" she said.

"I think you are very beautiful in the moonlight."

She held out her arms to me, forcing my face down again. I felt her hands tracing my sides, searching for something. And then she found it. "And how do you look in the moonlight, Dusky MacMorgan—more to the point?"

"Maybe. If you keep doing what you're doing, we'll see in a minute."

Diacona Ebanks was a young woman who knew no restraint. It wasn't a matter of taking turns pleasing the other, or demanding of the other. To her, lovemaking was just one long joyous experience to be shared. Shared again. And again. And again. She was like a young and perfect animal, happy to be free of all the social mores and rules of right and wrong. Naked beneath tropical night and above the midnight harbor, she reveled in this ancient freedom. She was like someone who because of some religious restriction was allowed to dance only once a year. But when she danced—look out.

"Do you like this, Dusky?"

"Umm . . . I like that just fine."

"I like it, too."

"In that case . . ."

I felt the weight of her lift and spread, heavy breasts oiled with her own labors. "Yes . . . that . . . only harder . . . yes!"

When we had finished it was nearing two A.M. by my Rolex. Boat lights in the harbor had gradually bunked out, leaving only moonlight and star paths upon the Caribbean Sea. She stood and returned with a damp towel. She wiped my body gently, kissing my back in the path of it.

"How does that feel?"

"Good. The wind's cool. It feels good."

"I have a whole week off, Dusky. I was born and raised here. I can show you everything."

"And I'm suddenly in love with Grand Cayman."

I felt her stiffen. "I don't like that word," she said.

"Grand Cayman?"

She chuckled. "No. Love. It's so . . . deceptive."

I pulled her head down to my chest and stroked her long dark hair. "You don't seem like the bitter type, Dia."

"I'm not. I'm really not. It's just that 'love' suggests permanence and disappointment all at once."

"It doesn't have to be that way."

"You sound awfully sure."

"It's a trick of mine. When I don't know what I'm talking about I try to sound sure."

"In that case, I'm not convinced."

"And in that case, I'm suddenly very much *enamored* with the Cayman Islands. . . ."

5

"Well, well, well, looka what the cat drug in!"

Westy O'Davis sat at the kitchen table of his cottage wolfing down a stack of toast and bacon. I could smell coffee. The light of a bright Cayman morning blew through the open windows. He wore gym shorts tight around his massive thigh muscles, and a loose open shirt.

"Sorry I didn't get a chance to scrub your floor this morning, Wes."

"Ah, it's okay, Yank. My wee Cayman cleaning lady did it, she did. Took some convincin', though. The superstitious kind." He paused, a chunk of toast hanging from his mouth. "You look tired, lad!"

"Only because I haven't eaten. Any more food in that refrigerator, or did you eat it all?"

"Eggs. Plenty of eggs, Yank."

"If I liked eggs I'd live in Iowa. I'll finish off this fish, if you don't mind. And fry some potatoes."

While I went to work in the bachelor kitchen, Westy outlined our plans for the day. He had already called Sir Conan James' secretary and made an appointment to see him and Lady James. Afterward, we would stop at Government House to talk with his adviser.

" 'Tis hard for an Irishman to say somethin' nice about the Crown, but they're efficient if nothin' else, Yank. Mighty efficient. And they might well have a line on the kidnappers. Sooner the better, I say."

Our schedule, O'Davis said, would leave us plenty of time to visit his dive-boat operation at Gun Bay Village, go over our equipment, and decide just what armaments we might need for a sea assault. If a sea assault was necessary.

Then he smiled at me and winked. "After that, Yank, you'll have the evening to yourself— if it was by yerself you spent last night."

"Are all Irishmen so nosy?" I chided him, turning the potatoes.

"Aye. It's in the genes. Every Irishman is secretly workin' on a book. Might even allow you a whole chapter to yerself, Yank."

"I'm honored. It makes me feel even more guilty about that clunker car of yours."

His ears perked. "Me car? MacMorgan, you didn't damage me fine little automobile now, did ya?"

Before I had a chance to answer, he went scrambling outside, pounding across the sand lawn like a country-boy fullback.

I followed him.

When he got to the car he smacked an open hand against his forehead as he surveyed the damage. "Ah, me poor sweet Bess, that American brute has damaged ya!"

"Bess?"

"An' looka the fender now, would ya! I suppose you were racin' one of the bloody islanders when you hit the telephone pole—admit it now, MacMorgan!"

"You call that ratty little red car 'Bess'?"

"An' looka the windscreen! You've shattered her bloody windscreen!" He patted the car fondly and gave me an evil look. "You'll not be drivin' me little automobile again, Mr. Dusky MacMorgan."

"If it always attracts the kind of attention I got last night, I don't want to drive the car, you crazy Irishman."

"Yer blamin' the car for the damage?"

So I told him about the silver Jag, and remorse for the car almost left his face.

"Shot at you, he did, eh?"

"Three times. Lucky for me he didn't follow up on it."

O'Davis tugged at his beard, thinking. "One person or two?"

"I only saw one. But he had me almost blinded with those damn bright lights. One man, I would say. Average height, very slim. Right-handed. Probably white, but I couldn't say for sure."

"Can't be many silver Jaguars on the island. My friend at Government House will be able to narrow it down. Until then, Yank, we have to assume the bloody fools were tryin' ta murder me. No one could have it in fer you after only a few hours on Grand Cayman." Then he smirked and smiled. "I figure it will take all of two or three days before the townfolk start shootin' at ya on yer own merit."

"Great," I said. "Thanks for the confidence."

After letting my breakfast digest for an hour, I borrowed a pair of goggles from the Irishman and went for my morning swim. The cottage porch opened out onto sand that sloped down to a natural bay created by the reef a half mile off shore. The bay was sky-colored, clear as gin, and I could see massive staghorn and brain coral through the transparent roll of waves.

I waded out waist deep, trying my best to avoid the spiny sea urchins. Then I swam with long, strong strokes toward the reef, feeling knots in shoulders and neck come undone. After my reclusive month on the stilthouse, I was in the best shape I had been for a long time. My weight was down, wind good.

Parrotfish scattered, then reassembled as I passed over. With every turn of head to breathe I could see a big barracuda trailing me, curious but keeping his distance. The color and splendor of the world beneath made even the tropical green sweep of Grand Cayman seem pale.

At the edge of the reef I turned. There was a natural channel through the forest of staghorn created by thousands of years of tidal stream. I timed the waves and sprinted on through. The water deepened on the seaward side of the reef, tapering down like the side of a mountain. In the blue-black depths I saw the shadow of something very large. Quietly, I sculled out to get a better look. It was a huge green turtle, broad as a butcher's block, but moving with all the grace of a predatory bird. Dia had mentioned that her family had been green-turtle hunters—like almost all the islanders in other times. The island economy had depended on those men in their native-built wind ships who sought the green turtle on the far and lonely banks between Cuba and South America. But when the world's turtle hunters began using engines rather than sails,

and as their hunting methods became more refined, the slaughter of an animal even as prolific
as the green turtle became too great. It was put
on the endangered-species list and hunting in
the Caymans was outlawed.

So this was one of the survivors I was seeing
now. He seemed unaware of his lonely position
as one of the few big greens left. Say what you
want about mankind, but you have to at least
admire our recent weak struggle to save what
we for so long only destroyed.

I watched the turtle until he flapped off into
the depths, then turned and swam back to the
cottage.

When I got there, O'Davis was still sweating
from his own workout. His shirt was off,
exposing waves of red hair on his weight-lifter's
chest. He wore a pair of tennis shoes, dirty
and frayed.

"Would ya like a beer, lad?"

"You have to ask? It's already after nine."

He got up and went to the little refrigerator.
"Believe I'll have a bottle meself. Walked the
beach last night an' drank a wee bit too much
of me fine whiskey. Sweated it all out, though—
ran clear up to Sparrowhawk Point an' back.
Beer's just the ticket now."

When he returned, he placed something else
on the table along with my bottle of beer.

"Am I supposed to carry this?"

"After the story ya told me, Yank, it might be wise."

On the gunmetal-colored grip of the little automatic was the famous banner: *Walther.*

"It's the PPK," O'Davis said. "Do ya know anything about it?"

"Just that it's pretty reliable because it's pretty simple."

"Aye. Blowback action, double-action trigger, and an eight-round clip. It uses 9mm shorts, and the boys at Government House tell me it'll drop a big man at thirty meters."

"If you can hit him at thirty meters."

"That's always the catch with these dainty little English weapons, Yank. But it's better than nothing, eh? I've got a harness for it so you can wear it under your jacket on the small of yer back."

"You don't mean suit jacket, do you?"

The Irishman had a twinkle in his eye. "Aye, an' what else?"

"I don't even own one."

He gave me an appraising look, like a tailor. "Ya kin borrow one of mine. Might be a little baggy on the spindly likes of you. But it's required. We'll be meetin' Sir Conan and his lovely wife at a little lawn party. And please at least comb yer hair, MacMorgan. Yer always goin' about in such a ragged state. Try ta put on yer best face in front of me gentry friends.''

Sir Conan James' Grand Cayman house was less a home than an estate.

It seemed odd to me that he would throw a lawn party little more than twenty-four hours after his son had been kidnapped.

O'Davis was less surprised. He explained as we drove toward the plush private-home section of Georgetown. "It's because ya do na understand the English that yer surprised, lad. Everything is stiff-upper-lip with them—especially the old English families. That wee island of theirs has done too well in too many wars ta let small things like a kidnappin' get them down. Besides, the way rumors circulate around this island, it's better they get their friends together in one spot ta tell them exactly what's goin' on.''

"You think Sir Conan might use the gathering as a chance to ask his friends for help coming up with the two million pounds?''

O'Davis thought for a moment. "It's a possibility," he said, "but I doubt it. Two million pounds is about four and a half million dollars, American. Wealthy as he and his ilk are, I do na think even they could liquidate that much in so short a time.''

"You'd think the kidnappers would have known that."

"Aye," O'Davis said, nodding thoughtfully, "you'd think."

The house was a monstrous white stucco structure hidden from the road by a wrought-iron fence and a brilliant hedge of hibiscus. A rolling lawn the size of a golf course had been landscaped like a tropical garden with bougain-villea, Barbados poinciana, and trees bowing with bananas, mangos, and sapodilla. A foun-tain, complete with marble statues, broke the road into a circular drive. A black servant in uniform waited to park our car.

"Now straighten yer tie, lad. Yer already look-in' a mess."

"You should talk, you big ugly potato head. Believe me, striped pants don't go with that red checkered blazer."

"Hah! Jest showin' yer ignorance about fash-ion, MacMorgan." As we came around the cor-ner of the house, people standing by the pool nodded at us without smiling. O'Davis lowered his voice and whispered, "Remember, let me do most o' the talkin'. Sir Conan is skittish when it comes to commoners. Especially American com-moners."

There were about twenty people roaming the

yard. A long buffet table had been set up beneath the shade of a banyan. Servants in white
jackets moved silently among the crowd car-
rying trays of drinks and snacks. Men and
women both were dressed stylishly: blazers and
summer prints and white open shirts. But there
was something missing from the party scene. I
couldn't put my finger on it at first. And then I
realized: no music. No games. No obligatory
laughter.

The people had divided into small groups,
caught in conversation. It wasn't a funeral atmosphere. Just subdued. More like old friends
socializing before church. Except for the alcohol.
The servants had to keep moving. The lawn-party
guests were dumping down the drinks pretty
quick.

We moved awkwardly along the crowded
deck. People gave us that quizzical "Nice to see
you—whoever you are" look. The Irishman
smiled back as if he were the host.

I grabbed a couple of drinks off a tray and
shoved one into O'Davis' hand. "Okay," I said.
"We dressed for the occasion—now let's get it
over with. Where's Sir Conan?"

"Yer always in a hurry, Yank."

"That's right. This tie's choking me, you look
like a used-car salesman from the Bronx, and
some little English kid's life is hanging by a

thread—other than that, I don't have a reason in the world to rush."

"Always time to admire the beautiful gentry ladies, MacMorgan. Like that pretty little thing on the other side of the pool. Only nineteen years old and stands to inherit a half million pounds the day she turns twenty-one. The Lord gave 'er a fine body, did He not?"

"O'Davis."

"An' how about the blond lady in that lacy white dress? A little older, true, but still a fine example of womanhood."

"O'Davis, I'm going to throw a bucket of cold water on you in about two seconds if you—"

"Okay, okay! You kin be a regular bully, do ya know that?" He surveyed the crowd with a delicate sweep of eyes. "There," he said. "Lady James is sitting in the shade of that fine big oak."

"And what about Sir Conan?"

"I figured I'd see him with one o' the pretty ladies I was viewin'."

Lady James didn't look up as we approached. She was lounging back on an outdoor divan. She wore a floppy white hat that hid the top half of her face from view. Her dress was long and sleek, like something out of a 1920s Fitzgerald novel. Her long pale legs were crossed demurely. In her right hand was a martini. A line of empty glasses trailed across the table by the divan.

"Lady James?"

She paused, then looked up. "Should I know you?" The smile was slightly drunken. "Yes," she said, "I think so." I guessed her age at thirty-five. Except for the eyes, she looked younger. I wasn't prepared for the classic porcelain beauty of her. Lady James had a face from a Renaissance painting. Only slimmer, finer: every detail of nose and lips and cheeks perfectly defined. Hers was a beauty you expected to be accompanied by a trail of broken, desperate lovers and all the hysterics, tragedy, and madness that the combination of great beauty and wealth often implies.

"I believe we met a week or two ago, Lady James."

She touched the hat brim back with a finger, her eyes focusing on us. "Yes," she said. "The award. You are the Irishman who was presented the medal."

"Aye, that I am. It is kind of you to remember."

"I suppose it is." Her eyes shifted to me. Her eyes were a watercolor green and her hair was the palest shade of auburn. She took a sip of the martini. "And what about your friend? I know we've never met. I would have remembered your friend."

"Allow me to introduce Mr. Dusky MacMorgan of the United States."

She held out her hand as if she expected me to kiss it. I took the hand in mine and shook it briefly. In the green eyes was an unmistakable look of invitation. The Irishman interpreted the same message, but recovered faster than I.

"We'd be here to see yer husband, Lady James," he said quickly.

"Conan?"

"It's about yer son, Tommy."

She sat up quickly. "You have some news?"

"I'm sorry to say we do not. I've only come to offer me services if they might be of some help."

She snorted and gulped at her drink. Her sarcasm couldn't be missed. "How kind. How very, very kind. We already have the entire island police force, two private investigators, and God knows how many helicopters and boats searching. But I'm sure if you just pin on that bloody medal of yours, you'll be able to find my poor little lost boy."

"I didn't mean to offend you, Lady James."

She wiped the corner of her mouth delicately. "No, I suppose you didn't." Her eyes caught me again. "And what about you, Mr. . . . MacMor-

gan, was it? Are you here to offer your services, too?"

"I suppose it beats getting drunk at a lawn
party."

Her eyes burned into me for a few beats, and
then she tried to get drunkenly to her feet only
to collapse back down onto the couch. "And just
what is that supposed to mean?"

"Read what you want into it."

"You'll have to forgive me vulgar friend,"
Westy interjected hastily. "Bein' from America
and all, with no education to speak of, he has a
tendency ta act like a brute upon occasion." The
Irishman gave me a meaningful elbow as he
spoke.

Lady James wiped her forehead with the palm
of her hand. She sighed as if about to cry. "No,"
she said finally. "No, he's right, Mr. O'Davis. I
was very rude to you. And I suppose one never
has the right to be rude." She looked at me.
"That was your meaning, wasn't it, Mr. Mac-
Morgan?"

"Sometimes you have the right and the reason
to be rude, Lady James. Under the circumstances, you're probably entitled to both."

"Charm," she said, smiling wearily. "You
have both temper and charm—a dangerous
combination. But I'm afraid you must forgive
me. These last two days have been a nightmare.

You're a man. You could never understand a mother's love. My son, Mr. MacMorgan . . . my son is the only thing in this entire ludicrous life that has made any sense. He is a wonderful boy. All the genius, the passion . . . the delicacy of an artist. And now someone has taken him from me. Can you understand what that means? The only thing in my life that I've ever truly loved, and now they've taken him. . . ."

Her voice had been rising steadily. I felt people watching us. She stopped just on the brink of hysteria, spasmed once close to tears, then downed the last of her drink.

"You're right, Lady James. I can't understand that. I doubt if anyone truly can."

Her smile was suddenly kind. "And maybe you understand more than I gave you credit for, Mr. MacMorgan."

"Maybe."

"Ah, Lady James," the Irishman interjected, "if you would jest point us toward Sir Conan, we'd be leaving you to yer guests."

"Well, speak of the devil," she said, an edge to her voice. "Here comes my beloved husband now."

He came trotting down the massive marble steps from the house. He wore an expensive short-sleeved shirt and pleated slacks. He was tall, with the build of a professional tennis

player. The black hair was wavy, close-cropped.
The face demanded a double take.

Lady James motioned toward him. "Jimmy!
Jimmy, come here, dear. These two gentlemen
would like to have a word with you."

Sir Conan James was the man I had hidden
from the night before in Diacona Ebanks' apartment.

6

Conan James possessed a quality of openness and mannishness backdropped by an air of aristocracy.

I'm sure that everyone he'd ever talked to in his adult life came away feeling the better for his friendship. Americans call that quality leadership. The Irish call that quality British. He had it all: strong handshake, congenial smile, look of concern, and that peculiar ability to make everything he said sound as if he was trusting you and you alone with the information.

Under any other circumstances, I would probably have liked him. Or at least not disliked him. But I kept seeing the look on his face when Dia refused him: a man trying to bed his mistress the night after his son was kidnapped. I tried my damnedest not to let him see the contempt I felt for him.

He led us inside to his study. The shelves were lined with books, and the furniture was plush, covered with saddle leather. There were mounted fish on walls of natural wood. The servant brought us drinks, then left without a word. Sir Conan sat behind his desk near the fireplace. There were French windows behind him, and it made it hard to see his face or read his expression. O'Davis and I sat in chairs that would have seemed more at home in some London men's club.

"Commander O'Davis—do you mind if I call you by your rank?"

"Wes is fine, Sir Conan. Or Westy."

"Fine. Wes, I appreciate your offer to help. Government House tells me that you requested this assignment."

"I had become friends with your nanny, Cynthia Rothchild. She was murdered in me home."

"Yes. Most unfortunate. A fine, fine person, Cynthia."

"Aye, she was. But I'd like ta make it clear, Sir Conan, that me interest is more than jest personal. I realize that a man in yer position is privy to much of the information that goes through Government House. You know that I do more than jest teach scuba divin' ta tourists.

I also serve Her Majesty in various capacities, but the less said about that the better. What I'm sayin' is, I volunteered because it is also me dooty—in a professional sense."

"And your friend?"

"Me friend is a friend—no more, no less. I asked him ta join me because he possesses certain abilities that could be invaluable if we are ta save yer lad."

"You know that many other people are working on the case?"

"I do."

"But you are intent on going ahead anyway?"

"I am."

He nodded and allowed us a conservative smile. "Good. I'm glad. You have my every confidence that if there is some way to free our Tommy, you will find it. But promise me this, Wes. Promise me that you will do nothing that will endanger his life if you do find him."

"I promise we will do the very best job we can, Sir James."

"I appreciate that. Now tell me how I can help."

"First of all, do ya have any intention of tryin' ta raise the two million pounds?"

"Quite impossible on such short notice, I'm afraid."

"In that case, we'd like ta see the lad's room."

"The police have already gone over it."

"Sure, an' I trust they found every scrap of evidence. But we'd like ta see it jest the same."

We followed him up a broad, winding staircase. The boy's room was like a little household unto itself. In one corner of the room was a table and sink with a marble top. There were Bunsen burners, racks of test tubes and chemicals and beakers. On the other side of the room was one of the most massive stereo systems I have ever seen. There were four speakers, all as tall as the average man. Special shelves had been built to house his hundreds of albums. French doors opened out onto a balcony. Near the windows was an ebony grand piano.

"How old is your son, Sir Conan?"

"Fourteen. Almost fifteen."

"And he still had a nanny?"

"More a tutor than nanny, Mr. MacMorgan. Lady James and I each have our interests. They often take us away from home for days at a time. We felt better with Miss Rothchild here. You see, Tommy is an extremely intelligent boy. His instructors tell me he is brilliant. The work he was doing in physics and chemistry was on the highest college level. Miss Rothchild was a great help."

"And music?"

Sir Conan smiled. "Tom is well schooled in

the classics. But like most teenagers these days, he loves rock and roll. We had this room sound-proofed because of his love—and our disdain—for it."

"What sort of burglar defenses do you have on the estate?"

He shrugged wearily. "Too few, obviously. Mr. O'Davis can tell you this island has a very low crime rate. At one time we had watchdogs, but their barking became a nuisance. There were burglar alarms, but my son usually slept with the windows opened—and always unlocked. So of course no alarm went off."

"Who was in the house the night your son was kidnapped?"

"Two members of my permanent staff—they've been with the family for years and can be trusted completely. Miss Rothchild, we had thought, and my wife. I . . . was away on business."

"Off the island?"

"No. Just away from the residence. As men, you can certainly understand."

Westy took over the questioning for a while. "Could ya be tellin' us who found the ransom note, Sir Conan?"

"The maid. It was pinned to Tommy's bed."

While the two of them talked, I made my way around the room. There was a photograph of the boy on the dresser. He looked frailer than I would have expected a son of Sir Conan James to look. He had his mother's translucent skin, huge dark eyes, and a bristling hair cut. There was no smile—just a look of distant interest, as if he were wondering what kind of camera the photographer was using. There was a shelf full of books on chemistry and natural science. I pulled a couple of books out and found the kid's secret cache of *Playboy*s stashed behind them— the sexual standbys of all adolescent males. The record albums were mostly rock and roll. Some Beatles and Rolling Stones, but mostly groups with names suitably bizarre: *Cannon Fodder*, the *Sex Pistols*, *Kiss*, and others. The covers get weirder with each progressive acne generation, but the volume and lack of artistry remain the same.

I went out on the balcony. Someone had removed the ladder. There were scratch marks on the wrought-iron railing. A high-powered telescope stood beside the railing. The lens cover was off and I peered through. It was aimed at the low northern horizon.

"Does your son wear glasses, Sir Conan?"

He gave me an odd look. "No. With all the reading he does, one would think he would have to. But his eyes are perfect. We had them checked recently."

While O'Davis asked him more about the ransom note, I completed my examination of the room. Two other things caught my attention.

"What time does Tommy usually get up in the morning?"

The Englishman thought for a moment. "He has private instructors while on the island, so he sleeps rather late. About nine, I suppose."

"Who sleeps in the room below this one?"

"No one. It's the guest room, and we've had no guests." It was obvious Sir Conan was getting a little tired of questions. "Really, Mr. MacMorgan, I don't see how any of this applies. The fact is, someone has taken my only child. If you two gentlemen really are interested in helping, then I strongly suggest you get out with the others and begin looking. This is a very small island. He has to be somewhere!"

For the first time, emotion crept into the man's voice. It was less anger than concern.

"You are absolutely right, Sir Conan." I looked at the Irishman. "Ready?"

"Aye, that I am."

He showed us to the front door and we both shook hands. Outside, the lawn party was still in subdued motion. While O'Davis went searching for his ratty little Fiat, I stood in the shade by the drive. That's when I heard a voice calling me.

"Mr. MacMorgan. Mr. MacMorgan, just a minute."

It was Lady James. She stood in the shadows at the corner of the house. There was a fresh drink in her hand. The long dress followed the lush curvature of her body perfectly. She had removed her hat, and the pale hair tumbled down on her shoulders.

"Yeah?"

She waited for me to get an arm's length away before she said, "I just wanted to apologize again for being rude. And to wish you luck."

"Thank you," I said. "We'll do our best."

She had the burning look in her eyes again, poorly hidden by her obvious nervousness. "And to prove my apology is sincere, I was wondering if you wouldn't dine with me this evening."

"If your husband—"

"Jimmy has other plans. Let me speak plainly, Mr. MacMorgan. The invitation is for you and you alone. There is a matter of greatest importance I would like to discuss with you."

I tried to shuffle for some excuse, but before I could, O'Davis came roaring up in his red car. "Good," she said, waving. "I'll expect you at nine. Dress . . . casually."

When I slid in beside him, O'Davis raised his eyebrows. "What was that all about, Yank?"

"Lady James wants me over for dinner to-night. And you're not invited."

The Irishman chuckled gaily. "Ah, I bet she does want ye fer dinner, lad. Served alone, *au naturel*. But I'm a little surprised she didn't invite meself as the main course. . . ."

Our stop at Government House was short and uneventful. Nothing more was known about the kidnapped boy. Police were following up a couple of leads, but they really didn't have much to go on. Every hour, Radio Cayman was reading a plea to the kidnappers at Sir Conan's orders. It asked them to contact a neutral party of their choice so they could negotiate. Lab reports had turned up nothing on the murder of Cynthia Rothchild—only that she had been killed by a very sharp instrument, probably a razor. Westy's English superior told us all this in a dry, bored voice before officially welcoming me to the case—his welcome made, I noted, with all the dubiousness he could muster.

The Irishman wheeled us back through the main part of Georgetown. Great modern financial institutions dominated the tiny town: Canadian Imperial Bank, Bank of Nova Scotia, Chase Manhattan, Swiss Bank and Trust, and many others. As a tax haven, Grand Cayman has become an important base for international finance and investment. As a result, barefooted island

children roam the streets hawking their wares
of conches and woven hammocks in the shadow
of billion-dollar money institutions.

O'Davis turned the car into Alice's Texaco beside the two-story gray-pink Cayman police station. Explaining, he said, "Need a bit of fuel.
While you wait, lad, I'll stop at headquarters
and ask me policeman friend about yer silver
Jaguar."

"And while you're doing that, I'll walk back
to the library."

"Is this any time ta be spendin' yer time in
idle readin'?"

"You never know," I said. "You never know."

The Cayman library was a squat conservative
building of stone block. The lady at the desk
was pleasant and eager to help. She went
through their books on astronomy and finally
found the star chart I requested. When I had
finished, I thanked her.

"Not at all," she said in the pretty mixture of
Scotch, Southern, and English lilt of the Caymans. "Anytime you need somethin', please
come."

When I got back, O'Davis and I crossed the
street to the Fort, a pleasant, informal restaurant
that served pretty good green-turtle steak.

"Did your policeman friend give you anything to go on?" I asked as the waitress brought us our iced tea.

"Aye. An' somethin' very interesting too. But first, tell me—what was that business about goin' to the library, Yank?"

"Simple," I said. "The kid's telescope. It wasn't focused anywhere close to infinity—as it would be if he had been recently viewing constellations. Furthermore, I checked the star charts. No planets rising in the north this time of year. So why would he have it pointed that direction in the first place?"

"Could be jest accidental, Yank. Maybe he moved it."

"You're right. But we're looking for any lead we can get.

"True, true."

"Furthermore, the telescope came into pretty good focus on the landward horizon. Sir Conan said the kid had perfect eyes and that means average. My vision was something better than average last time I had it checked. So what's directly north of Sir Conan's estate?"

The Irishman thought for a moment. "Boatswains Bay, maybe. Somethin' near the point of North Sound."

"Is it a secluded area?"

"Some of it is. The turtle farm is out in that

direction. An' the little settlement I told ya about—Hell."

"A couple of other things in the room caught my attention. Behind one of his bureaus someone had drilled a hole. I doubt if anyone else noticed it. Scrape marks on the floor tipped me off. One of the drawer legs was sitting right on top of it."

"I wondered why you were movin' the furniture."

"When Sir Conan had guests, I think his little Tommy was peeking at them."

"I've somethin' of the voyeur in me too, Yank. What does it prove?"

"Probably nothing. I'm just trying to put information together. You pile up enough random information and before you know it a picture emerges. The picture I'm getting of Tommy is one of a very intelligent kid who also has a very active interest in sex—like most people over the age of twelve. But put the two together. Sir Conan is a womanizer. You told me that yourself, plus I got some firsthand proof which I'll tell you about later. His mother is a beautiful drunkard who has the look of a nymphomaniac in her eyes. Tommy is more than smart enough to understand what's going on. But kids are funny. What they fantasize about for themselves seems repulsive when they see their parents in some sexual role."

"What are ye tellin' me, Dusky?"

"I'm telling you there's a chance the kid just got mad and staged his own kidnapping."

"Aye. But it doesn't account for the murder of me poor Cynthia."

"That could have been a completely separate incident."

"Sure, it coulda been. But that doesn't explain one thing."

"What's that?"

"There's only one silver Jag on the island."

"Who owns it?"

"When I met me Cynthia she was drivin' a rental car because hers had been stolen. She never mentioned what make. The police still haven't found it. It was a four-year-old XKE. And painted silver."

7

Even after O'Davis told me about the thirty-foot
workboat he used to carry his diving parties out
to the reef, I didn't expect the old wooden
clunker that was moored off Gun Bay Village
on Cayman's east end.

"Pretty little thing—fer a powerboat—don't
ya think, Yank?

"Yeah—pretty like a bulldog."

"And jest what is that supposed to mean?"

"Don't they sell any paint on this island?"

"Paint! Now would ya have me ruin the natural beauty of 'er?"

We stood at the edge of East Sound, looking
out toward sea. The water was so clear that the
boat seemed to hover over the coral bottom in
midair. What paint there was was white and
streaked with rust. The cabin had been built far

forward, leaving no bow deck. Behind us, kids played in the sand yards where chickens scratched. Windfall mangos rotted beside colorful ply-board houses, and women on the streets carried parasols to protect them from the March sun.

The Irishman jammed his fists on his hips and *humphed* loudly. "I'd be havin' a prettier vessel ta squire ya around in if I hadn't a lost me fine sailin' ship savin' yer snitty little life back in Mariel Harbor, Cuba."

"God, you've got a memory like an elephant."

"In that case, you'll not be bad-mouthin' me little boat again."

"Deal."

Big black letters on the stern of the boat proclaimed its name: *Rogue*. O'Davis paddled us out in a leaking tender that threatened to sink beneath the weight of us both. Once aboard, he anchored the dinghy off.

"It'll take us all day to get to the other end of the island in this thing—not that I don't like going slow," I added quickly.

"Will it now?" he said slyly. "We'll see." Humming his strange Irish tune, O'Davis went below to the cabin and returned with something heavy wrapped in oilcloth. He laid the package on the deck and unrolled it.

"Fast or slow," he said, smiling, "we'll be well armed."

There were two old Thompson submachine guns—the kind you see in the old gangster movies, but without the circular drum magazines. These had the standard box clips.

"Always carry them for sharks," he explained. "Both of 'em work good as new. Thirty-round clips for each with about four hundred rounds of .45 caliber stashed below."

"I take it you have a lot of sharks around here."

"Never had ta shoot at one." He grinned.

I was wrong about O'Davis' old dive boat being slow. And I was ready to admit it the moment he fired up the engines. The whole superstructure trembled with the loud *burple* of mufflers.

"It's not diesel?"

He shook his head. "Twin GMC 442s. Awful hard on fuel, Yank, but this ol' boat will fairly scream across open water."

And scream the boat did. I unclipped the mooring line, feeling comfortable once again after changing out of that damnable suit. O'Davis maneuvered us skillfully through the reef, pointed the bow west and north, then drove both throttles home. The force of it jerked my head back and I had to grab hold of the bulkhead to keep from being thrown overboard.

"Slow, ye said!" the Irishman cackled. "An' do ya call this goin' slow?"

"Not too bad—for an older boat, that is."

O'Davis grimaced and put all his weight on the throttles. There were long glassy swells rolling out of the north. Gulls and a stray cormorant flapped madly out of our path while coral heads through the clear water went by in a blur. The old boat rattled like a skeleton, but the engines ran perfectly. Every wave brought teeth crashing against teeth, jarring the kidneys. We were doing at least fifty.

And fifty in an old thirty-foot boat is fast. Very damn fast.

"Okay, okay," I yelled. "I'm convinced. You have a quick boat. Now slow down before you kill us both."

Laughing happily at his victory, the Irishman backed down a quarter on the throttles. "Fastest boat on the island," he said proudly.

"Why is it I keep thinking this hull wasn't made for twin four-four-twos?"

"Ah, she does shake an' shimmy a bit. But she's like an old wife—jest complains ta let ya know she's around. The hull's seen a decade or two come an' go, but she's made of native mahogany and manchineel—sound as a dollar."

We ran just off the reef line past Wreck of

Ten Sails, where, according to O'Davis, a fleet of Jamaican merchantmen bound for England had misunderstood a warning light and, one after another, grounded on the reef on a dark night in 1788. A couple of other rusted hulks, oil barges, sat partially submerged off Roger Wreck Point.

"This wee island has seen the world's sailors and pirates come an' go in the last four hundred years," the Irishman mused. "An' some o' them that came never made it away again. No one will ever know how many vessels rest broken below that bloody reef line. Divers find new ones every year."

We skirted the island and headed west toward North Sound. The landmass was lush and green, edged with white beach across the expanse of turquoise water. Twice a helicopter angled across the island in front of us—part of the search for the son of Sir Conan James.

"On an island as small as this, ye'd think it would be very hard to hide anything—let alone a human bein'," O'Davis said. "But as ya kin see, Yank, there's a lot of untouched swamp and jungle on Grand Cayman. That's why I wanted ta take ya fer this little ride."

The Irishman was right. Traveling by car, I had gotten the impression that you were never far from a road or a house. But once past the eastern point of the island and the sparse settlements of Gun Bay Village and Spotter Point, there were nothing but desolate expanses of beach backdropped by palm trees leaning in windward strands and the deeper green of tropical forest.

The only other boats to be seen were some kind of barge—a dark smudge on the rolling horizon—and a large sailboat, outward bound.

A few miles north, we began to see more houses. O'Davis rummaged through the little dunnage box and handed me a chart of Grand Cayman. It was weathered, soft as tissue, and there were rum lines with compass headings showing wrecks and reefs penciled in.

"We're coming up on Old Man Bay now?"

"Aye. An' that's Grape Tree Point jest ahead. There's only one road connectin' the south side of the island with this—the north side. If I was wantin' ta hide, I'd try to disappear west off that road."

"The chart says it's pretty high ground."

"Locals call it a mountain. O' course, it's not really a mountain; more a series of bluffs than anything. The only real mountains are below us. All submerged. The island herself is a part of the Cayman Ridge, a range of submarine mountains which extend from the Sierra Maestra range of Cuba westward to the Misteriosa Bank toward British Honduras."

"Very interesting, professor."

The Irishman grinned. "Part of me speech to the tourist divers."

"And a good speech it is—but I want to know more about the inland bluffs. A person really could hide there for a time without being found?"

"I'm afraid I'm not well schooled on the mountain. Few islanders are, Yank. All sounds very romantic, explorin' bluffs, an' all, but when it comes right down to it, the sun's hot and the rocks are sharp and it's about as easy as walkin' through a thousand acres of brambles."

"Then that seems the place we ought to search."

"An' what do ya think the helicopter is for, mate?"

"They can see everything from the air?"

He shook his head. "No—not everything, certainly. There be caves up there. Nobody knows how many fer sure. Back in the seventeen hundreds Edward Teach used one of the caves as a hideout. Somethin' of a tourist attraction now. Some say it was where Teach shot his first mate, Israel Hinds."

"I remember the story. *Treasure Island*. And Teach is known as . . ."

"Aye. Blackbeard. The pirate Neal Walker came to Grand Cayman a few years later. History says he robbed the galleon *Genoese* of sixteen thousand pieces of eight. Legend says he buried it somewhere on the island."

"And that's another part of your speech to the tourists?"

"They do warm to the idea of buried treasure," he said, smiling.

At Rum Point, Grand Cayman's even shoreline suddenly gave way to the ragged, massive indent of North Sound. The Irishman banked southward along the tropical wilderness, leaving the tourist traps like Cayman Kai behind.

I was beginning to find it all very discouraging. For an island only twenty miles long and eight miles wide, there was one hell of a lot of open shoreline and an equal amount of inland forest. And we didn't have much time—only thirty-six more hours, if the kidnappers stuck to their word. It seemed like an impossible task. We needed more to go on. It was a time for fast work, and following hunches if need be. But I didn't even have enough information to form a hunch.

"What were you and Lady James talkin' about when I came up in the car?" O'Davis asked suddenly.

"She invited me to dinner—but I already told you that."

"It's jest that you mentioned you knew Sir

Conan to be a womanizer. It's a popular topic of conversation with her. But she usually waits until she knows ya a bit longer—an hour or so."

"No. She didn't tell me. It came from some accidental original research I was doing."

He tilted his head in question. So I told him about my meeting with Diacona Ebanks and the scene in her apartment.

"Could have been rather awkward, Yank, had he seen you—bein' invited to his lawn party and all."

"I got the impression that he would have acted as if it had never happened."

"Aye, ya might be right. Most Englishmen got a skin like an elephant. Robots."

"You think Sir Conan might have been involved with Cynthia Rothchild?"

"It crossed me mind. I mentioned it to her two days before she died. She got quite huffy. She said absolutely not. Hard to imagine Lady James letting her stay had they been makin' the creature with two backs."

At Governors Creek we passed a fleet of native-built commercial boats where, for four hundred years, the turtle ships have been kept at anchor. Black men, sweating in the sun, worked in the rigging and wove nets. Ratty houses in the background were painted bright blue and conch pink. Some of them still had roofs of thatch. An emaciated dog stumbled through the March heat, looking for shade.

O'Davis nodded toward a hatchet-shaped point of land beyond.

"That's Head of Barkers. Ya wondered about the landward horizon ya saw through the telescope."

"That's it?"

"Aye. That an' the little curve of peninsula before ya get to West Bay."

"Can you get in a little closer?"

"We'll slip in through the reef at the point an' run right up the shore."

The Irishman pointed the old boat in, and at a heart-stopping forty miles an hour we rode the surf toward the reef. As accustomed as I am to running coral shoals, I didn't see the narrow cut between the deadly staghorn until we were right on it. We banked left, then right, on a twisting path that took us safely in beyond the surf line, then ran parallel between shore and reef over the white sand shallows. A big ray exploded off before us, and a couple of sharks were black shapes lancing off at an angle.

"Houses out here are mostly islanders," O'Davis explained as we roared along. "The turtle farm is down around Boatswains Bay, an' they have a wee school, too."

"But Tommy James had a tutor?"

"Aye. Cynthia. And he attended one of the private schools back in England, I suppose. One o' them places where bloodlines are considered before grades and hasn't closed since the Vikings invaded." The Irishman thought for a moment. "But if the lad was ta have island mates, I suppose most of them lived out here."

"But other English kids live on the island, don't they?"

"Sure, sure. A brattish lot, fer the most part. Money does it to 'em, I suppose."

"Or maybe it's just that you're Irish and can't be expected to be impartial."

"Possible," he said wryly. "That's jest possible."

Ahead, the sprinkling of small houses gave way to a ragged coastline of volcanic rock that protruded from the surf like teeth. Upon a bluff above the shore a rolling lawn and fence were shaded by a stand of ironwood trees. Through the trees you could see the well-manicured geometrics of a large estate.

"I thought you said all the houses out here were owned by islanders."

"I said most o' them were. Still some big houses from the old slaving days."

"Who lives there?"

The Irishman shrugged. "Don't be expectin'

me to know everythin'. I thought the place was deserted. Used ta be."

It wasn't now—that was obvious. Someone was walking through the shadows of the trees.

"You have any binoculars aboard?"

He produced a pair from the dunnage box and handed them to me. By the time I got them focused, the person was almost to the house. It was a man. Probably a very young man—although he was too far away to tell for sure. He was slim, wore shorts, and had long blond hair. He paused at the side of the house—the garage. The door slid open mechanically, then closed almost immediately.

"Damn!" I said.

"An' what's the problem, Yank?"

"There was a car in the garage, but I didn't get a good look at it."

"So?"

"So it was some kind of small car. I didn't get a long enough look to see what make. But it was silver. I'm sure of that. And if I had to guess, I'd say it was a Jaguar."

8

On the trip back, we decided to do some preliminary checking on the house through official channels and, if we didn't get the proper answers, to make our own investigation.

At midnight.

The journey back to Gun Bay Village didn't take long. O'Davis got his *Rogue* outside the reef and drove the throttles—and us—home.

As I showered, O'Davis made some telephone calls. And then I made a call of my own.

Dia Ebanks seemed delighted to hear from me. And then not so delighted.

"Dusky, I really shouldn't even talk to you!"

"I left a note."

"Yes, and what a note," she complained in her pretty Cayman accent. "I'll read it: 'Diacona, sorry I can't spend the morning with you.'

That's it! No explanation, no promise to call. Honestly, I've never felt more like a one-night stand in my life. I've spent the whole day thinking of nasty things to say if I ever saw you again."

"Well, I promise you'll get a chance to say them—but maybe not tonight."

"What?"

"Dia, I'm afraid I'm going to be tied up most of the evening on business."

"Planning a new charter business on Grand Cayman, right? Dusky, you know I don't believe that for one minute. If you don't want to see me again . . ."

"Dia, I want to see you again. And again and again. I want to spend time with you; get to know everything about you. But I can't. Not tonight."

"Not even very, very late tonight?" There was a wistfulness in her voice that was touching. "I need something to look forward to, Dusky. The man . . . who came to my apartment last night called. He's had a very terrible personal tragedy. His son was kidnapped—but you don't want to hear about that. The point is, he called and said he needed someone to talk to. But I refused. Can you imagine how hard that was to do? I turned him down because I knew I would be seeing you. Dusky, please."

"If I can, Dia. If I can."

O'Davis had his best lecherous grin on when I hung up. "Lady problems, Yank?"

"You might say that."

"It's quite the busy calendar ye have for the evenin': Lady James at . . . nine, was it? And then yer pretty mystery girl, an' then a house-breakin'."

"Wait a minute—you checked on the house?"

"Aye. Remember I said I thought it was deserted? It's supposed to be. The place was owned by a rich Canadian. He died a year ago an' the estate is still tied up in the courts."

"Then who did I see this afternoon?"

He shrugged. "That's what the police are very anxious ta know. Had ta pull some strings to get us the first look. But it wasn't the caretaker. The caretaker is a black fellow named Onard Cribbs. Apparently no family ta speak of—not on Grand Cayman. He's Jamaican."

"So we go at midnight."

"Aye."

"Can you get us some aerial photographs of the place?"

"I kin try, Yank. The next question is, shall we go by land? Or sea?"

"If I was a kidnapper, I'd have a watch posted on the road and the gate. So it might be a nice night for a swim."

O'Davis smiled. "Nothin' like bathin' by moonlight."

At nine on the dot I arrived at Lady James' seaside estate. There was a servant at the gate. He nodded without expression as he let me pass in O'Davis' little red Fiat, as if used to such intrigue.

Earlier in the day we got word that the kidnappers had been in touch with Sir Conan.

Sir Conan's secretary, more correctly. The contact had been made by telephone. The sound of traffic in the background suggested it was a pay phone. O'Davis had gotten a full report from his man at Government House, complete with a tape of the call.

He had played it on his little cassette recorder while I listened from the tiny kitchen, steaming lobster we had caught that afternoon.

Because the call had been unexpected, the tape began midway into the conversation.

". . . Sir Conan James?"

"No. This is his secretary."

"Then listen and listen good. The message won't be repeated. The boy is safe. But we won't hesitate to kill him if you try some sort of silly rescue. We want the two million pounds in used notes. You will package them in a waterproof container. You will harness the container to a

parachute. You will prepare a small plane with
a loran—"

"We need more time," the secretary interrupted. "Tomorrow is Sunday. We need an extra
workday to negotiate with the banks—"

"Shut up! If there is another outburst, I will
hang up and we will kill the boy! You will have
the money and the plane ready by Monday before midnight. You will attach a green flare to
the parachute. Our next communiqué will be
by marine radio, channel zero-six. Understand?
Someone must monitor that channel continu-
ously. When the time is right, we will give you
the loran coordinates at which the plane will
drop the money. We will have put the boy adrift
in a seaworthy skiff. You will find him within a
mile of the drop site. We will radio you the exact
loran coordinates once we are safely away."

There was an odd clicking sound and then the
voice of an adolescent boy came onto the line.
It sounded as if he were talking from a tunnel.

"Father? Father, this is Tommy! I am quite
well, but please do exactly what they say! They
will kill me if you don't. I know they will!"

And then the phone went dead.

The Irishman had switched off his cassette recorder. "What do ya think, Yank?"

"The guy calling was obviously trying to dis-
guise his voice. Tried to make it deeper,

rougher. I'm not sure if the English accent was real."

"Aye. I believe it was. And so do the lads at Government House. Broad vowels of Lancashire. Most mimics affect the Cockney adenoid. I'd say he's English, most certainly."

"It sounded as if he was reading his demands point by point. But he gave us another day without hesitation. But was it because Sir Conan's secretary asked for it, or was it because *he* needed it?"

"Whatever the reason, Dusky, we kin use the time."

"Yeah, but the point is, if he gave us the extra day because of the secretary, it means he's the boss man. He's the one who makes the decisions. And why not send some flunky to a pay phone to make his demands?"

"Maybe he jest doesn't trust anyone else."

"Or maybe there is no one else. Maybe it's a one-man scam. Maybe that's why he was so insistent no rescue attempt be made."

The Irishman thought about it for a while. He smiled wryly. "Yer a shrewd one, Yank."

"And I might be entirely wrong. What was Sir Conan's reaction when he heard the tape?"

"Lads at Government House said he actually broke into tears when he heard his child's voice."

"Then there's no doubt it was Tommy. But didn't the sound of his voice strike you as odd?"

"I figure the kidnapper taped the lad's voice and played it back over the phone."

"Yeah. Yeah, that's it. He couldn't risk taking him into Georgetown. And it accounts for the hollow sound." I had plopped the six big lobster tails on plates, using tongs, then added drawn butter and island lime. "So does Sir Conan still want us to visit that deserted house tonight?"

"After hearin' the kidnapper's threat, he was reluctant. Very reluctant. But they made it plain that if he could not pay the two million pounds, we had to act."

"So it's still on?"

The Irishman nodded. "They also made it very clear, Yank, that if the boy is there and we don't think we can get him out cleanly, we should return and confer with the police."

"But there won't be any cops around, right? We don't want to take any chance of tipping them off."

"They agreed—a bit reluctantly." The Irishman had cracked the tail ungraciously with his bare hands and dipped a chunk of the sweet lobster in the butter. "Need I add, Yank, that much is riding on our shoulders? Me adviser at Government House has no girth of faith in the two of us—probably because I'm Irish and yer ugly. Seems to think I'm tryin' to turn this inta a private vendetta because they murdered me little Cynthia."

"Aren't you?"

And he had grinned, chewing the fresh lobster. "Aye, that I am, lad. But let's keep that a secret between jest us two. . . ."

So I arrived at Lady James' as promised, anxious to get her feelings on the kidnappers' demands. And just as anxious to find out more about this strange family: a playboy baronet, his drunkard lady, and their genius son who had sounded so small and desperate on the cassette tape.

I motored up the drive and through the tropical gardens as the servant closed the gate behind. The white mansion was shadowed by trees, glowing in the moonlight.

I got out of the car, feeling involuntary sexual stirrings low in my abdomen. There had been a touch of nymphomania in Lady James' insistent invitation. There was little doubt why she wanted me to visit with her husband away. And I was playing the roll of a very straight, very disinterested American detective.

So why had I washed my hair and shaved until my skin burned, and then dressed in soft cotton khakis and light-blue chambray shirt?

For the later meeting with Diacona Ebanks?

That's what I told myself. But something deeper within me knew that I was lying; knew that, in a subconscious sense, the paper-pale skin and the aristocratic lengths and contours of Lady James might be just a little too attractive to pass up. There was something about her attitude of sovereignty that would make any man want to muss the soft hair and rip the expensive clothes away and reduce the aloof and regal beauty of her to the basics of a naked man and a naked woman grappling beneath covers.

I rapped the brass knocker twice, and the huge doors swung open. An older woman, complete with apron and English maid hat, stood before me.

"Lady James is expecting me."

She nodded, not even bothering to hide her disapproval. "This way, sir."

I followed her up the winding staircase. The house smelled of fine wood, leather, and books. At the top of the stairs, she led me down a hall to a room with twin doors.

"She's waiting for you," she said unceremoniously. Like the servant at the gate, I thought, the old maid had been through this little charade many times before. And suddenly, I felt a tinge of self-disgust. I knocked softly.

"Dusky? Is that you?"

I swung the door open. It was a large dark room with French doors that looked out onto the sea. Moonlight came through the windows, and candles flickered beside the bed. Somewhere a stereo played something soft and complicated with strings and timpani. There was a bottle of wine in a silver ice bucket. Lady James lounged on a mound of pillows on the round bed. Her hair was over one shoulder, pale as spun glass. She wore a sheer nightgown without frills. Her breasts were small and firm, the nipples dark and erect beneath.

"I was expecting dinner."

Her smile was remote, with just a touch of the cat. "Were you? How quaint."

"I'm new to the island. I take invitations at face value."

There was an empty wineglass in her hand. She brushed fingers through her thick hair and stretched. "Perhaps I should have been less . . . delicate."

"Or more honest."

"You struck me as being very intelligent, Mr. MacMorgan. Please don't tell me I was mistaken." She purred the next words. "I would be very, very disappointed."

"There's always the butler. You do have a butler, don't you?"

Her delicate face hardened momentarily. She

slid off the bed and poured herself another glass of wine with the calculated movements of someone who is slightly tight. The nightgown came down to her thighs and moonlight filtered through it. Her ribs were shadows swelling into the ripe curvature of hips and the curled blond mane of sheath.

She sipped at the wine, her lips wet. She smiled that same remote smile. "Then let me be plain, Dusky. You are very big and very strong, and I would like you to take off your clothes and make love to me. You may treat me as you will—like the lowest whore in creation, if you like. I want you to love me as if it will be our first and only time—because it most assuredly will be." There was a wryness to her smile now. "And if you came here looking for information, information you shall have. But afterward. And only afterward. . . ."

9

In one motion, she put down the wineglass and stripped the gown up over her head. There was a brief flattening of breasts as she lifted her arms, then she shook her hair back into place.

"Those are my conditions," she said.

She walked through the moonlight toward me and took me in her arms. I found my head tilting downward, finding her mouth with mine, feeling her thighs spread to push herself against me while her fingernails traced their way up and down on the inside of my leg.

She was pulling me backward, backward toward the bed. And then I was lying beside her as she worked feverishly to unclip my belt. She smelled faintly of perfume, and her tongue tasted like the wine. There was an animal want-

ing about her; that uncontrollable drive to couple, seed, and be done with it.

She was having trouble with the belt. It gave
me some much needed time to think. I've got
this pious streak in me. Maybe it's there to help
me think I'm a little more moral than I really
am. Or maybe it helps me rationalize the on-
and-off loves I've indulged in over the last few
years. Whatever the reason, it's there. It was the
source of the wave of self-disgust I felt welling
up inside me now.

Sure, it would have been very, very easy to
bed the pretty aristocrat and moan and groan
in fleeting ecstasy—then somberly shake hands
afterward. Another job well done by yours truly,
Dusky MacMorgan. And wasn't it part of the
job? She had said as much. If I wanted information then I damn well had to please her first.
Just put it on the voucher; that expense account
of conscience to be filed away and forgotten.

And the thought of that revolted me even
more.

I found myself disentangling myself from her
arms for the same reason I work out every day
and meditate every day and watch the diet: because the mile swim makes the beer taste even
colder, and the meditation makes the world
seem a little more orderly, and the diet makes

the allotted steak and potatoes seem better de-
served.

The *Playboy* philosophy of sex for sex's sake
only serves to deaden the bedmanship with one
you really care for.

And going a few rounds with the beautiful
Lady James would have cost me a hell of a lot
more than I would have profited, because it
would have poked a hole in that thin veneer of
self—the fragile armor we all wear to keep out
the cold, cold universe and the uncomfortable
truth that we all are nothing more than the briefest fleck on the endless flow of humanity.

I stood up. There were candles on the stand
beside the bed. I stood in the flickering light and
slowly unbuttoned my shirt. She lay back naked
on the bed, touching herself, watching me.

"I can't," I said.

She sat up quickly. "You what? My God, what
can you possibly . . ."

I had the shirt unbuttoned. I pulled it back,
turning the scarred side toward her. One long-
gone night in the Pacific, I had had a near-
deadly run-in with an oceangoing dusky shark.
He wasn't supposed to be in those waters and
he sure as hell wasn't supposed to attack.

But he did. I made it to shore with the help
of a friend, and lived to wear a massive half-

moon scar that circled from pelvis down toward my thigh; that and a new nickname.

I saw her face contort when she saw the sheen of the white mauled flesh.

"Do you understand?" I repeated. "I can't."

"My God," she said in a small voice. "I'm sorry. I didn't know."

"I was stupid to let it get this far."

"But isn't there anyway you could . . . you could just please me?"

And suddenly the naked Lady James, all moist and perfumed, was no longer beautiful. Or even passably attractive. The selfishness of her last question made me see her as she was: a pathetic, lonely creature in a woman's body. And to her, I was nothing more than a vehicle of pleasure. A nonentity. A life-support system for the phallus cure-all she desperately wanted.

"Sorry," I said. "If I tried, I'd be miserable for a week."

Her disappointment was plain to read. "Oh. Beastly awful—a man as lovely as you in such a fix." She got quickly to her feet, went to the massive closet, and wrapped herself in a bath-robe.

"I'm not too wild about it myself."

"How did it . . . happen?" The question couldn't hide her sudden boredom.

"I'd rather not talk about it."

"Ah. I see."

So I was trading one lie for another: the lie
that I was physically unable to serve as her me-
dicinal stud. She fiddled with a box on the
nightstand, found a cigarette, and lit it, inhaling
deeply. "Would you like a glass of wine before
you leave?"

"No. But I would like to ask you a few
questions."

The ash of her cigarette glowed bright orange.
She studied her watch suddenly as if she were
late for an appointment—or as if gauging how
much time she had to find a replacement for
me. "Yes. Of course. But couldn't it wait until
the morning?"

"Fine," I said. "Sure. Your son has been kidnapped by a person or people who think nothing of slitting a woman's throat, and you want
to wait until tomorrow to help."

She glowered at me through the candlelight.
There was a new coarseness in her voice. "Who
do you think you are, talking to me in that fashion? Who do you think you are!"

I waited and said nothing.

She gulped down the rest of her drink, then
poured another. She looked at me unsteadily,
her eyes burning. "You feel contempt for me.
Isn't that right? My poor little Tommy is gone,
and you think I should be wringing my hands

and crying and praying—well, I have been! But rest assured I will never lower myself to perform in front of your kind! So I tried to get you into my bed. And why not?" She inhaled savagely on the cigarette. "I am familiar with your type, MacMorgan. You can be useful—in bed or in war. But for what else? Men! You men have such inflated opinions of yourselves. But what am I saying? I called you a *man.* You can't even claim to be that. Can you? You're nothing but a big beautiful eunuch. And a detective, no less. Why, you should have become a hairdresser!"

I wasn't exactly prepared for the sudden hysteria. It showed on her face and in her eyes.

"Apparently, your husband isn't much better—if you have to invite total strangers to your bed."

Her grin was malicious. "Ah, clever ploy, MacMorgan. Such a clever way to spur me into conversation about my dear Jimmy. That was your intent?"

"That's right."

She nodded and slopped more wine into her glass. "Excellent. All right. I'll tell you. Sir Conan James. Another beautiful man—like yourself. Only much smarter. And with much loftier antecedents. Impeccable breeding. Sterling background. A very old English family, always looked upon with trust and favor by the Court."

"So why the sarcasm?"

"Sarcasm indeed!" She snickered merrily. "And what could prompt such sarcasm? He was a picture student at Sandhurst when we met. Brave on the rugby field, and then fearless in the service of our country. He did all the proper things in the proper ways with never a breath of scandal to soil his precious family name."

"And just what the hell is that supposed to mean?"

She smacked her hand down on the nightstand. "It means he has been very bloody shrewd! Don't pretend you don't know, Mac-Morgan! Everyone on this whole bloody island knows about my husband! He likes the ladies—that's what they all say. And such innocent wording: 'He likes the ladies,' indeed!"

"And you like men."

Her face described wonder. "Can you blame me for cuckolding him? Can you? You have no idea what it has been like. Every place we have ever been, he has had a half-dozen mistresses. Or more. He gives them presents, he pays them—whatever it takes." Her voice lowered. "And then he has to buy them off."

"Blackmail?"

She lit another cigarette, her voice even wilder. "I wish. How bloody easy that would be! Can't you understand—*my husband likes to hurt them.* He builds up to it. Just as he built up to it with me! It is his sexual technique; the only way he can be fully satisfied." She used her hands theatrically. "Ah, but you haven't seen my scars, have you? Actually, I have only a few—on my back, mostly. He at least had the good grace to wait until after Tommy was born. That is why I have my own room. And my own locks. And my own lovers." She took a gulp from the wineglass, her hand trembling. "Do you see, Mr. Dusky MacMorgan? My husband, the much honored Sir Conan James, is quite totally insane."

"Does your son know?"

"Who can understand what a child knows? My God, I hope . . . I hope . . ." Her voice trailed off in sadness. And then: "I used to worry, you know. I used to have this awful dread Tommy would grow up to be like his father."

"And what makes you think he won't?"

For a second I thought she was going to throw the glass at me. Instead, her voice took on a new hoarseness. "Because my son is *perfect.* Perfect, do you understand? There is a gentleness in him. A kindness that would forever forbid such madness."

"I see."

She stood up unsteadily and walked across the room. "Now, dear eunuch, if you have learned quite enough, please leave me." She swung the door open, a frail pale-haired woman with skull-like eyes in the strange combination of moon and candlelight.

"One more thing, Lady James."

"Yes?"

"Your husband's women—are you even the least bit jealous?"

She snorted with sarcasm. "Jealous? And what wife wouldn't be?" And then she shook her head. "Mr. MacMorgan, all I feel for those women is pity. A very great pity. The thought of my husband makes me feel ill. . . ."

And suddenly, I was in a very great hurry to get to Seven Mile Beach and the Sea Mist Apartments where Diacona Ebanks lived.

If what Lady James said was true, Sir Conan James had more than a touch of the sadist in him. And he had called asking if he could talk with Dia, and Dia was all too alone. . . .

I floored the Fiat, skidded through the open gate and out onto the road. I had to keep reminding myself to drive on the left side. The Fiat started missing and popping and complaining when the speedometer hit fifty.

I checked my Rolex. Nine forty-seven.

Traffic seemed heavy. And then I realized that it was Saturday night.

Drivers on Grand Cayman are always erratic. Every curve in the road is a challenge, and every hill a promise of something exciting just over the rim.

But with the added number of drunks on the road, driving was an honest-to-God war.

I took my time maneuvering through George-town, almost collided once with an old Volvo speeding through a stop sign, then floored the Fiat north on the seaside road which parallels Seven Mile Beach. All the tourist traps and gaudy hotels and restaurants were alive with neon and parking lots jammed with cars. Back in America's Midwest, it was still a sloppy, freezing spring. But here in the tropics, it was vacation time; the months for Ohio's and Indiana's mass of diving and fishing enthusiasts to head for the Caribbean.

I roared down the road—and right past Dia's apartment complex.

A small green sign proclaimed: *Sea Mist Apartments.*

I ground the Fiat into reverse, backed up, and then spun into the visitors' parking space.

We all have premonitions and unspoken dreads. We see tragedies that are about to happen—but usually don't.

But on those rare occasions when our premonitions are right, we congratulate ourselves on our perception, and assure ourselves in our deepest heart of hearts that we *can* see into the future; that the course of our lives is all pre-ordained.

And I didn't like the premonition I was getting now.

I slammed the door of the Fiat behind me and went running up the stairs, three steps at a time.

I pounded on the door once. Twice. And still no answer.

"Damn!"

And I was just about to run for a telephone and the police, when someone's eye covered the peephole, and the door swung open.

"Dusky!"

It was Diacona. Her smoke-brown hair was parted in the middle and hung down over her shoulders. She wore soft bleached jeans and a gray blouse. There was a paperback book in her hand.

"Dusky, what is it? You look flushed."

I moved past her as she shut the door behind. "Must be the tropical climate."

She smiled and hugged me. Her hair smelled of shampoo. She demanded a kiss before any conversation. I was happy to oblige. I had felt emotionally grimy after my near miss with Lady James. All the hatred in her, all the madness, seemed to cling to me like a bad odor.

But now I felt better again. Dia looked fresh and unspoiled; free of the psychological wear so many women crumble under.

"I guess I was worried about you."

"Um . . . that's a good sign. It means you care for me. I offer this as a token of my appreciation."

Her lips were full and moist.

"You taste fine," I said.

"And you do, too," she answered sleepily. But then her eyes blinked wide open. "You . . . you taste like lipstick! And not the kind I wear!"

I laughed. There was such a look of childish outrage on her face that I couldn't help it. "That's because I was kissing another woman earlier."

She backed away from me, hands on her hips. "What a nerve you have. The least you could do is lie about it!"

"Did I ever tell you that I love your Cayman accent? It's like a combination of French and Scottish. It might be the prettiest accent I've ever heard."

She kept backing away. "No, no . . . don't you try to flatter me now."

"You don't want me to tell the truth and you don't want me to flatter. Then how about if I just tell you a story?"

She stopped and looked at me seriously. "Dusky, what's this all about?"

So I told her. I told her why I had come to Grand Cayman—without going into the specifics. And I told her how I knew Sir Conan James and about my earlier meeting with his wife.

And when I had finished, she was stunned. She sat on the couch with her hands folded in her lap for a long moment. "And he always told me that *she* was the crazy one," she said incredulously.

"He was right. She is. But maybe he is, too." I hesitated, then decided to tell her what had been worrying me. "Do you remember hearing or reading about the woman who was murdered a few days ago?"

"Yes," she said, her mahogany skin growing suddenly pale. "It was just awful. She had had her . . ."

"Throat cut," I finished. "She was the friend of a friend of mine. He says she wasn't involved with Sir Conan. I'm beginning to suspect otherwise."

"But Jimmy . . . Jimmy is no murderer!"

"You don't know that, Dia. How long did you say you've known him? Only a few months?"

She nodded.

"Was he ever . . . unusually rough with you? Did he ever seem to enjoy hurting you?"

"Dusky, that's very embarrassing . . . me telling you about the way it was with him."

I put my arm around her. "I know. But believe me when I say it doesn't matter. I need to know."

She thought for a moment. "There were times when he seemed to go a bit far. But I . . . I . . ." She turned her head away from me. "You know, I rather like it that way sometimes."

"No, Dia. There's fun. And then there's cruelty."

She wiped at her forehead. "Now that I think about it, it seems he had been getting a little more extreme—but only lately. I had to ask him to be gentler a few times. And then the way he talked to me the other night while you were here. That seemed very unlike him." She looked at me quickly. "But Dusky! You don't really think Jimmy killed that poor woman, do you?"

"The police have no suspects, Dia. He's the only one who even comes close."

"But what could that possibly have to do with the kidnapping?"

"I don't know. Nothing is making any sense. I do know that under no circumstances should you let Sir James into your apartment again. Understand?"

She nodded, close to tears. "To think . . ."

"Do you have a weapon? A gun around the apartment?"

"Why, no. I've always hated the things. Don't even know how to operate one."

I went outside to the Fiat and got the Walther O'Davis had given me. With the clip out, I showed her how to use it. I made her fire a dozen dry rounds. Then I demonstrated how to arm it.

And when I stood to leave, she fell into my arms. "Dusky, stay. Please stay. I'm so frightened. . . ."

I kissed her softly on the forehead. "I can't. Not tonight."

She wrapped her small hands in my hair and pulled my face down to hers. Her lips parted, tongue searching, delicately exploring.

"I need you," she whispered.

The buttons of her blouse strained as my right hand moved up her ribs, cupping the weight of her.

"But I can't."

Her hands began to move. There was the slow metallic sound of a zipper.

"I won't keep you. Not for long. If you say you have business, I believe you. And if you say you escaped Lady James, I believe that too." She moaned softly. "Why is it I believe everything you say?"

My left hand stroked her hair. I turned my wrist and checked the Rolex. It was ten twenty-three. I was supposed to meet O'Davis at eleven.

"Must be my honest face."

She tugged at my belt, and the khaki pants began to slide toward the floor.

"Oh," she whispered, "look what's happening."

"I have to leave in a half hour. I mean that. No matter what."

"Then we had better hurry, Dusky darling," she said huskily. "I moved some cushions out onto the patio. There's a party going on down in the harbor, and we'll be able to see the lights and hear the music from the patio. Hurry, Dusky. Please. We don't have much time. . . ."

10

As planned, I met the Irishman in Hell.

But despite my promise, I was twenty minutes
late. Diacona Ebanks had a way of making you
forget time. With boat lights throwing yellow
paths across the night harbor, we had joined
again in a frenzy of love and wanting. She was
the best of lovers: a woman whose reserve fell
away with her clothes.

*"Oh, Dusky, that was wonderful. It's never been
like that before."*

"And you are one very special lady."

"Then promise me you will come again."

"Is this a new game of puns?"

And she had laughed softly in the harbor
quiet. *"Yes. I feel so delicious and wicked. Promise
me—you will return tonight."*

"It may be very, very late."

"I'll give you a key. Just slide into my bed beside me. Promise?"

"Okay, Dia. I promise. No matter how late. . . ."

So I raced the little Fiat along the seaside road of Seven Mile Beach toward West Bay. The road narrowed, the Miami Beach–style hotels slowly thinned out and became small island houses. Huge land crabs moved with ghostly precision across the asphalt as my car lights funneled through the darkness.

At a giant bend, the road diverged. Rocks jutted from beneath the brush and undergrowth in the moonswept night. A white sign acknowledged I had arrived:

HELL

I smiled in spite of myself. I always knew this day would come—but I never expected to be at the wheel of a Fiat with thoughts of love fresh in my mind.

Ragged houses lined the road. There were coconut palms in the yards. Windfall mangos added a cloying sweetness to the warm March night.

The club Inferno was a gray-and-white concrete building built on a slab. A dozen cars sat in a jumble upon the shell parking lot. A neon sign in the window promised Red Stripe beer.

A handpainted sign at the door warned: *Enter at Your Own Risk—It's Hell Inside.*

At least the people of the little Grand Cayman settlement had a sense of humor.

The windows of the club vibrated with music. The jukebox was turned up high. I went through the door into the loud laughter and the haze of cigarette smoke. The record playing was a clatter of steel drums and island voices: *Work all day, work all night—daylight come an' me wanna go home. . . .*

Black and mulatto faces turned to stare as I entered. A couple of them nodded their welcome, then went back to their laughter and their conversations.

The Irishman sat at a table by an artificial fireplace. There were photographs of cricket teams on the wall, and a wide-eyed devil mask. Across from him was an older black man with huge shoulders. The black man wore baggy clothes and the kind of sweat-stained hat you see in 1930s detective films.

O'Davis checked his watch as I took a seat. "Bit late, aren't we, brother MacMorgan? Did ya get waylaid, now?" He cackled at his own joke, and the black man laughed.

"Business, you big ugly Irishman. Strictly business."

"Ah, course it was. Course it was. Dusky, I'd

like ya to meet me neighbor and friend, Mr. Hubbard MacDonnel.''

He had huge hard hands, knobby with labor. "I was askin' him about the night poor little Cynthia was murdered," O'Davis said. "Tell Dusky what ya told me, Hubbard."

Hubbard MacDonnel had a thick Cayman lilt. He was given to wide gestures and an infectious grin. But the most striking thing about him was his eyes—he had pale-blue eyes, evidence of Grand Cayman's tolerance of all the early sea-blown races which had taken harbor on its shores.

"Didn' hear much, mon. Not much. An' ol' Hubbard don' miss a trick, neither." He wiped his mouth with the back of a huge hand, then took a gulp of his Red Stripe. "Heard a car slow, then turn inta Mr. O'Davis' drive. An' I thought, 'Well now, this is very fine. Westy's gettin' home early for once, maybe done with all the crazy weekday drinkin'. Kill a mon, it will.' "

"And that's all you heard?"

He shook his big head and smiled. "Ain't done with the story, see? Then I heard *another* car comin'. But this don' sound like Westy's car. Sound deeper. Bigger engine. This car turn, and I think, 'That big Irishman, he given up the liquor for a pretty island lady. An' that worse for a mon than strong drink!' " He laughed gaily.

Hubbard MacDonnel finished his beer with another long gulp and gave the bartender a circular wave of the hand, asking for another round. When it arrived, he continued. "Few minutes later, I hear somethin' else. Maybe a cat lookin' for romance. Maybe a scream. Then I hear the car with the deep engine race back toward Georgetown. Next mornin', constable comes. Says this English woman has been murdered. He asks me the same questions as you." The old Cayman man smiled again. "I figures Westy done kilt her, so I tell the constable nothin'. Didn' want to get so crazy an Irishman in jail over a woman!"

"Ah, kind of you, Hubbard, kind of you—but I didn't kill the lass."

"Know that now, man. Didn' know it then!"

O'Davis checked his watch. "Dusky, I'm thinkin' it's time fer us to get goin'."

"One more thing," I said. I looked at Hubbard. "You know anything about a Jamaican named Onard Cribbs?"

He looked at O'Davis, as if he preferred the question came from him. The Irishman nodded. "Cribbs," said MacDonnel, the contempt easy to read in his voice. "Yeah, I know that Onard Cribbs, mon. Flathead Jamaican nigger, what he is. Jamaicans hate the Queen." He tapped himself on the chest proudly. "We here love the

Queen—that the difference, mon. Onard come
to dah island maybe year ago. Runnin' ganja.
Marijuana. Cocaine. Who knows what else. Bad
mon, that Jamaican nigger. Constable get him
once, then let him go."

"Why?"

Hubbard shrugged. "Don' know, mon. Constable tell him get a decent job or get the hell
off Cayman. Onard get a job as caretaker up the
road a piece at some big estate. He come in here
sometime, but not for long. Us islanders run him
out. Even so, we stay away from that estate he
care for, mon. Onard one nasty flathead nigger!"

Hubbard insisted on paying the bar tab, and
the Irishman and I left throwing promises over
our shoulders that we would come to his house
one afternoon for plantain and green-turtle stew.

Outside, O'Davis and I climbed into the
cramped Fiat. He backed out onto the shoulder
and headed down the twisting road toward
North Sound.

"That's a pretty loyal friend you have there,"
I said.

"Hubbard is a fine old man. Salt of the earth,
ol' Hubbard. Employed him aboard me old ship
when I had a spot o' work ta do fer the government. Very handy with his hands, and knows
how ta keep 'is mouth closed. Fancied 'imself

somethin' of a secret agent after the job. An' he's my eyes an' ears when it comes to the island folk. Come ta look upon him as me second father."

"Good choice," I said. "It always surprises me when you show good taste, O'Davis."

"Hah! An' how kin I argue that when I have the likes o' you sittin' beside me, ya dirty little snit!"

While we headed for his boat, which he had brought around from Gun Bay Village to the west end of the island, I told him about my visit with Lady James, and about my suspicions concerning Sir Conan James.

"Some of it adds up when you think about it," I said. "Let's say, just for argument's sake, that Sir Conan was having an affair with his son's nanny, Cynthia Rothchild. Then you came along. He gets jealous. And then he follows her. It just so happens that you're not home. He goes inside and there's an argument. Sir Conan has a sadistic streak in him. But this time it goes too far. He rips her blouse. She grabs a knife to protect herself, but he takes it away and uses it to murder her."

"But Yank, she tol' me she wasn't havin' an affair with him."

"Some women lie as good as or better than

men. Sir Conan wasn't home that night—remember? He was away when his son was kidnapped."

"But what about the fella in the Jaguar? How would Sir Conan get hold of Cynthia's stolen car? If he's as crazy as his wife says he is, I kin understand why he would take shots at me—but how did he get the bloody car?"

I wiped my face with an open hand. "Hell, I don't know. Maybe the murder and the kidnapping and the attempt on your life are all separate occurrences. Maybe one doesn't have anything at all to do with the other. Or . . . damn . . . I don't know." I looked at O'Davis. "I should have known that if you wanted help it wouldn't be anything easy."

"An' would I need help if 'twas?"

"One thing's for sure—tomorrow, we have to tell your police friend to put a tail on Sir Conan. I don't like him running around loose."

"Yer worried about yer stewardess friend?"

"And wouldn't you be? There's somebody on this island with snakes for brains—and, so far, the arrow points to him."

"I'll tell him," O'Davis said with a shrug, "but Sir Conan is a very powerful man, brother MacMorgan. They'll not be pickin' him up on jest my say-so. They're goin' ta need some proof."

"Just so long as they watch him."

The road took us east across the narrow peninsula of island. There were shapes of small houses and stone fences. A night heron flapped off through the blaze of headlights, a crab squirming in its beak. The roadsigns were round and plain, peppered with buckshot. Australian pines leaned feathered and frail by moonlight. Through a crevice of trees, the water of North Sound spread away from the land, silver and swollen.

"You brought my gear?"

"Aye, that I did."

"The knife, too?"

The Irishman nodded. "Yer nasty-lookin' Randall knife, too. . . ."

Bota Bano is a little fishing settlement which, for four hundred years, has watched the explorers and the pirates and the green-turtle hunters come and go. Wooden piers reeled drunkenly into the night sea. Commercial boats were black smudges on the harbor. House lights shimmered across the bay. The place smelled of diesel and hemp. While the Irishman changed clothes, I tested his handheld 200,000-candlepower light. The beam knifed through ten feet of clear water to the coral sand bottom. Sergeant major fish froze in the white glare at the base of a piling. There were beer bottles on the bottom and a rusted fifty-gallon drum. Amber antenna of a half-dozen lobsters protruded from the drum, and a large strawberry grouper rested with heaving gills and malicious eyes.

"We'll not be needin' the light, I'm thinkin'." O'Davis came out of the cabin, pulling at the zipper of his black wet suit.

"You're going to run that little reef cut blind?"

"It's either that, Yank, or let them know we're comin'."

"In that case, I'll say a few Hail Marys while I dress."

"Didna know you were Catholic, Yank."

"I'm not—but I figure you are. Or once were."

Traveling across the night water at forty miles an hour, the shoreline seemed to move—not the boat. I wore my lucky Limey knickers, rubber dive boots, and a black watch sweater. O'Davis hummed his strange Irish tune as he stood at the wheel. The moonlight added a rusty halo to his red hair, and his beard fluttered in the wind.

We rounded Head of Barkers staying well away from the reef. There were no house lights now, and the shore was a dark haze of coconut palms and Australian pines in the distance.

"Should be the Canadian's estate jest ahead."

"And the cut through the reef?"

"Up another quarter mile, I should think."

"You think? Christ, you're going to kill us on

the coral before we even have a chance to search the house."

O'Davis cackled gaily. "Hah! Wurra, wurra—ye've got more Irish in ya than Scotch, Mr. Dusky MacMorgan! Jest leave the drivin' to me."

"But you can't see a damn thing!"

"I can hear, Yank. I can *hear*. Now jest give me a few minutes' silence!"

Surf breaking over the reef was a writhing gray line in the moonlight. The ratty cruiser, *Rogue*, lifted, paused, and nose-dived in the stern sea as we powered toward shore, twin props cavitating at the peak of every wave. Then, suddenly, I could see the narrow surf break of the channel.

And O'Davis was right—you could hear the difference. Even so, it wasn't something I would have tried with my beloved *Sniper*.

He drove the wheel hard to port, banking west, brought her halfway back, then hard a-starboard.

The cruiser took a wave over the bow in a warm sheet, there was a heart-stopping jolt as a staghorn crushed beneath us, and then we were free, on the landward side of the reef.

"By sound, huh?"

"We made it, didna we?"

"I'll go below and see how big the hole is."

"Hole? Hah!"

O'Davis was right. The coral had not damaged the hull. In the weak cabin light, I checked
the planking for leaks and found none. Upon
the vee-berth rested the two Thompson machine
guns, oiled and lethal.

A quarter mile from the Canadian's estate, the
Irishman dropped the cruiser off plane. The
sound of the surf was off to our right now. I
got the anchor ready and dropped it when ordered. In the new silence, you could hear the
wind in the pines. It leached a warm citric odor
from the land.

You could barely see the neat geometrics of
fence and well-kept lawn in the moonlight.
There were no lights on in the house.

"Doesn't look like anyone's home, Yank."

"We'll see," I said. "We'll see."

"We've got a short swim ta shore—maybe
two hundred yards."

"Good. We'll swim on our backs and carry
the weapons. Remember, if something goes
wrong and we can't make it back to the boat,
we'll meet at the car."

"Aye."

The Irishman wore mask and snorkel. I opted
for just the good Dacor fins. The water was
warm, with a current that swept east toward the
point. Far off, I could hear the diesel rumble of

a boat headed toward North Sound. It ran without lights. I swam on my back, propelling myself with long languid strokes of fin. Ahead, there was a loud swirl and watery *whoof* as some predatory fish crashed bait.

I remembered the sharks we had seen earlier. But my Navy SEAL training had long ago dulled my fear of night diving. We had done almost all our patrols in Nam at night. You become a fatalist: If a shark wants you, he's going to get you. So why worry?

It had taken me a long two months after recovering from my own shark attack to regain the relaxed attitude of the fatalist and be comfortable again.

Even so, night is the time for the blue-water killers to come feeding on the reefs. Everything fears them. And they fear nothing.

We made it to shore okay. My clothes were wet and warm and soggy. I waded backward over the jagged rocks, checking each step before putting full weight down because of the poisonous black-spined sea urchins.

We hid our dive gear in the brush by a line of coconut palms. I had my knife, a small narrow-beam flashlight, and the Thompson. O'Davis carried two extra clips in a waterproof pouch. He removed the clips and hid the pouch with the rest of our gear.

"Should we spread out when we get ta the fence, Yank?" O'Davis asked in a whisper.

"No. We've got plenty of time. Besides, I don't want to take the chance of you shooting me by mistake."

He snorted in the darkness. "If I shoot ye, Yank, it won't be by mistake!" His soft laughter blended with the sound of the surf.

11

The boat surprised me.

O'Davis saw it first.

We had made our way through the moonlight down the rocky stretch of coast. The estate was perched upon a bluff with a twenty-foot sheer ledge. We were looking for a place with plenty of handholds so we could make the climb.

And that's when he saw it. He grabbed me by the shoulder. "Looks like we might have company, brother MacMorgan," he whispered.

I followed his finger toward the dim shape anchored off a set of wooden steps that led up the bluff. It looked to be a small powerboat, sleek with the common flat racing design of ski boats.

"That wasn't there this afternoon."

"Yer a smart one, MacMorgan."

"If I was smart, I'd be back in Key West having my third cold beer after a supper at the El Cacique."

"I'll buy ya a better supper and colder beer when we're done here, mate."

"That's a deal."

We stood motionless and watched the boat for a long time. When we were sure no one was aboard, I slung the Thompson over my shoulder and climbed the bluff, digging into salt-damp crevices with knees and toes. The steps that led to the sea would have been easier to climb—but also a hell of a lot easier to see in the moonlight.

I pulled myself over the ledge and crawled to the nearest clump of trees before standing. Across the lawn, the house was huge and pale in the shadows. A wrought-iron fence lined both sides, stopping at the seaward bluff.

There were still no lights.

We stayed close together, moving from tree to tree in the milky light. Night birds squawked and palmetto rats scurried high in the trees. There was the distant whine of a jet and a starry spasm of flight beacons as a commercial airliner descended toward the island, bringing more tourists on a late flight from Miami.

At the back of the house, we hugged the wall, listening.

Nothing. Not a sound.

"I fear we've come on a wild goose chase, Yank," O'Davis whispered.

"Maybe. I just want to get a look at that car in the garage."

We slipped around to the side. I tested the garage door quietly. It was locked. I motioned with my hand, and the Irishman followed me to the front of the house. Something bothered me about the windows of the house—and that's when I realized what.

They were dark, all right.

Too dark. Far too dark for a moonlit night. Someone had covered them—from the inside. A very strange thing to do.

The front entrance was a formidable gate of two huge doors with a giant brass latch. The thin hand of illumination that came from beneath the doors told me what I wanted to know.

Someone was inside, all right. And they sure as hell didn't want anyone to know they were there.

"I think we're on to something," I whispered.

"Aye. But if me friend Hubbard was right, we may have jest stumbled onto a drug deal."

"Could be. Or maybe they have the kid. We have to get inside and see. There were some French doors at the rear. I should be able to jimmy the lock."

Silently, we returned to the backside of the

house. I used my Randall knife. I pried at the lock, jamming the blade between the doors. The windows weren't covered here—they had blacked out only the front part of the house. When the lock snapped, I opened the door an inch or so and slid my hand carefully up and down the edge of it, looking for a wire that might trip a burglar alarm.

There was none.

I put the knife back in its scabbard and stepped into the darkness of the house, Thompson submachine gun at hip level, ready.

O'Davis was a huge crouching shape behind me.

We were in some kind of den. The furniture was covered with sheets. The place smelled of mildew and old books. As my eyes adjusted, I could see the plasticine shapes of mounted game fish on the wall. The dead Canadian had been a "sportsman."

It was a huge house. We made our way through a dark maze of hallways, through the linoleum expanse of kitchen, to another hall illuminated by the filtering light from the front room. We could hear faint voices now. Soft laughter. Animated conversation.

We ducked back into the kitchen quickly when a shape covered the hallway and came our way.

O'Davis and I waited on each side of the open doorway. I took my knife out, poised and ready.

There was the sound of a door slamming. A long pause. Then a toilet flushed.

The figure returned up the hall to the front room.

"We've got to get closer," I whispered. "We've got to hear what they're saying. If it's about drug running, we'll get the hell out and leave it to the police. If it's about the kid, we'll take them."

"But not until we hear where they have him," the Irishman warned. "Can't take a chance of gettin' the lad killed."

I nodded. O'Davis was right. We had to take our time, plan our moves, and be very, very damn careful.

This was no time for a cavalry charge. Maybe the murderer of the Irishman's lost lady, Cynthia Rothchild, was among them. But taking his life in revenge wasn't nearly as important as saving the life of the kid.

"We'll move down the hall, room to room."

O'Davis nodded in the darkness.

The Irishman went first. When he motioned, I slid through the weak hall light, leapfrogging to the next room. It was a huge house. More furniture covered with sheets, more wooden crates. We moved noiselessly. What sound we did make was covered by the animated conversation in the main room.

At the end of the hall we ducked under a massive staircase. We could hear the voices clearly now. I held up an open palm toward O'Davis, telling him to stop. I waited for another outburst of laughter, then poked my head around the base of the stairs.

There were six men sitting around a massive oak dining table. A huge Canadian flag, red with white maple leaf, hung over a stone fireplace. There were charts hung on the wall, and more mounted fish. A layer of dust seemed to cover everything but the table.

A black man with a shaved head and a red scarf around his neck sat at the head of the table. His facial features suggested some Spanish inbreeding. He wore a Fu Manchu mustache and a handful of gaudy rings.

He dominated the conversation. Probably Onard Cribbs, the Jamaican that Hubbard Mac-Donnel had told us about. He had a sinister look about him: a smile that was more of a sneer and wild, unbalanced eyes.

The other five men were a ragged mixture of American and Jamaican accents. The guy with the long blond hair I had seen walking across the lawn looked to be about twenty-one, the youngest at the table. He had a prunish, feminine mouth and a row of bad teeth. Another white man sat beside him. Strictly American: expensive slacks and shirt with *Playboy*-style gold chains and flat computer watch. His face, crenellated with old acne scars, was shadowed with bluish stubble—the kind of beard that demands shaving three times a day.

These two sat together. They seemed nervous, anxious. Their laughter was forced. They shared a pack of Winstons, chain-smoking and stabbing the butts out in a heaping ashtray. A six-pack of Bud sat on the table, two cans left in the plastic harness.

The other three men were black. They wore ragged colorful clothes and no shoes. Two of them had the red, yellow, and green flag of Ethiopia sewn on their sleeves. The other wore no shirt. They all had bushy braided beards and long marled hair rowed into dreadlocks.

There was little doubt the three of them were Rastafarians, the Jamaican political/religious cult that preaches black supremacy, violence, and the daily use of marijuana. They call it the Wisdom Weed.

They passed a huge joint between themselves, never offering it to Cribbs or the two whites at the table. Their eyes were glazed, like huge black marbles. Their bag of ganja sat atop a long-barreled .357 on the table before them.

A friend of mine from Kingston had told me once about the Rastafarians. This was years after he and other hardworking blacks like him had been chased off that cesspool of an island by the thieves and lunatics. At the turn of the century a Jamaican named Marcus Garvey appointed himself the prophet of the black race. He predicted the birth of a black Messiah and the return of his followers to their homeland, Africa. He said his followers would inherit the earth— at the point of a gun. In the 1930s, the coming of a black king to Ethiopia, Haile Selassie, seemed a fulfillment of the first of Garvey's prophecies. The blacks living in abject Jamaican poverty embraced him as a god. They began styling themselves after Ethiopian warriors, with hair braided into spiked vertical strands using animal dung as an adhesive, and smoking the Wisdom Weed.

They refused to work—for themselves or anyone else. And as poverty increased in Jamaica, so did the Rastafarian following. And so did crime. Theft became a way of life, and the murder of a white or a non-Rastafarian was hailed as a step toward Haile Selassie's prophecy of black unity.

I felt my breath coming soft and shallow.

If these were the kidnappers of fourteen-year-old Tommy James, he would be killed ransom or no ransom.

I looked at O'Davis. He nodded, the resignation plain on his face. He knew what we were up against. I made a calming motion with my hand. He nodded again. There was nothing to do but wait and listen.

"So it's all settled then, eh, gentlemen?" It was Onard Cribbs. His shaved head mirrored the light from the overhead lamp.

"I think so," said the white man in the expensive clothes. The crispness of his voice couldn't hide the apprehension in his voice. He obviously didn't like doing business with the three Rastafarians. "If the rest of the goods are of the same quality as the sample, then we will pay your . . . friends three hundred thousand cash upon delivery." He hesitated. "But I want Dirk here to test it before loading, if you don't mind."

One of the Rastafarians looked up quickly. The other two paused in their smoking, eyes registering something lethal. "You no trust us, mon?"

"It's not that. It's just—"

"We can sell this heroin somewhere else, mon! Don't need your shit, see?" The spokesman for the Rastafarians had a high raspy voice, thick with Jamaican accent.

The guy in the expensive clothes lit another cigarette and gave Onard Cribbs a nervous look, asking for help.

The black man with the shaved head stepped in, the smile more of a sneer. "Gentlemen, let's not argue this late in the game, eh? Mr. Morro, you say your transport boat is offshore waiting?"

The man in the expensive clothes, Morro, checked his watch. "It should have arrived half an hour ago. Just off the reef line."

I remembered the diesel engines and the ship without lights I had heard on the way out.

Onard Cribbs looked at the Rastafarians. "And I know the merchandise is here, because I helped unload it last night. So what's the problem, gentlemen? A simple transaction, no?"

"Just don't want no shit, mon."

"You have to understand that Mr. Morro has his investment and his investors to protect—"

"Don't give a damn about his honky investors, mon! He either want the stuff or he no want the stuff!" The Rastafarian's speech was loud and incoherent. Quietly, the black man beside him had been inching his hand toward the .357.

Morro noticed. "We want it," he said quickly. "We want it. You'll get your money after the stuff is loaded."

"Want it before, mon. Want to count it before. Then *you* load it."

Morro was perspiring. Onard Cribbs seemed to be enjoying the scene. As middleman, he had nothing to lose and everything to gain.

I ducked back in behind the stairs feeling only disgust. It was becoming all too clear that we had stumbled onto a heroin deal, plain and simple. They had made no mention of the kidnapped boy. And we had given them plenty of time.

It was time to retreat. It was time to let these modern-day pirates go ahead with their deal. We would leave it to the Cayman police force.

But there was one more thing I wanted to check.

That silver sports car in the garage. Someone had taken shots at me, and if it was Onard Cribbs, I wanted to know why.

Using hand signals, I told O'Davis to stay. His expression asked why. He was as anxious to get the hell out as I was. I made a steering motion with my hands. He nodded his understanding.

I waited until they began arguing again before moving. I slid down the hall to the kitchen. It smelled of rancid grease. I stopped, trying to get my bearings. It seemed like the garage entrance should be right off the kitchen.

It was.

The door was swollen. It creaked as I swung it open. There were no windows on the garage door, and the place was pitch black.

I reached into the pocket of my commando knickers. They were still wet. I screwed down the lens cap of the little flashlight. It threw a concentrated beam. The garage floor was made of cement. It was piled with junk.

In the corner by the door were two wooden crates. The top of one of the crates was jimmied. My curiosity got the best of me. I lifted the top completely off.

In the crate were a half-dozen plastic sacks. They were stuffed completely full, like kapok in a cheap flotation jacket.

With my Randall knife, I sliced one of the bags open. The heroin came pouring out, as white and soft as flour.

One by one, I knifed the other bags.

If we were lucky, the Americans and the Rastafarians would spend enough time arguing over who had done it to give the Cayman police a chance to get here and arrest them tonight. It might have been a silly thing to do, but I felt frustrated—frustrated because I had seen the car.

It was silver. And a sportscar.

But it wasn't a Jaguar. It was an old Mercedes.

And it seemed to clear Onard Cribbs and his associates of any involvement in the kidnapping of little Tommy James and the murder of Cynthia Rothchild.

I was about to go back into the house and get the Irishman. It was time for us to get the hell away; to leave these drug runners to the cops.

But that's when I heard the heavy *ker-whuff* of the .357 in rapid fire. And then the hair-raising screech of a dying man.

12

I dropped the flashlight and unslung the Thompson submachine gun.

I went running through the darkness of the garage, tripped, fell, and was immediately on my feet again.

I could hear animated voices. Loud Jamaican accents. I didn't take my time now. And I didn't worry about making noise.

I went crashing through the kitchen and down the hallway. Then I could see the Irishman still hiding behind the staircase. He was motioning wildly at me. And then I realized they hadn't been shooting at O'Davis. They had obviously gotten into a fight among themselves. And O'Davis was telling me to be quiet; to hide and let them fight it out.

But it was too late. They had heard me coming. One of the Rastafarians crossed the distant space of the hallway, crouching when he saw me. I saw his arms jump as the .357 exploded. Plaster stung my face. I dove, rolled, and came up firing. The sound of the old Thompson made my ears ring. The Rastafarian went jolting backward, crashing through a window.

Realizing we had no alternative but to fight it out, the Irishman jumped from his hiding place.

"Freeze! Hold it!"

"Bust, mon! Goddamn cops!"

Another of the Rastafarians appeared from behind a chair with a clear shot at the Irishman. I had just hit the mouth of the hallway at full sprint. His sudden appearance startled me. But my unexpected arrival distracted him just long enough to save O'Davis.

I crashed into him in midstride, knocking the revolver out of his hand. He went down with a hoarse *whoofing* noise. There were more gunshots, answered by the deafening rattle of the Irishman's Thompson. I had the Rastafarian on his back. He grabbed for my weapon, trying to wrestle it away from me. He had his head tilted back, trying to bridge me off. I hit him with an overhand right flush on the Adam's apple, putting my weight behind it.

His eyes bugged and he clawed at his throat.

And then he lay still.

I heard the sound of crashing glass and jumped to my feet in time to see Onard Cribbs disappearing through a shattered window.

O'Davis raised his weapon to fire. I grabbed the barrel and shoved it away.

"There're enough corpses around here," I said.

His big Irish face was flushed with combat. He nodded his agreement.

There were, indeed, enough bodies.

The blond kid with the bad teeth, Morro's chemist, rested his head upon the table as if asleep. The pool of blood in which it rested said he would never wake up.

"They planned on killing them all along," the Irishman said thickly. "Cribbs had to be in on it. Even I could see it coming."

"The Rastafarians?"

"Aye." He motioned to the floor where Morro lay, his chest a spongy mass of crimson. "No great loss, killin' the likes of him. They shot 'im when he stood ta shake hands, closin' the deal. The blond kid didna get a word out before they shot 'im. Figured I'd jest let 'em go about killin' each other till you came crashin' in. Kind o' glad ya did, Yank."

The Irishman had killed the third Rastafarian. He was sprawled in a heap on an overturned couch.

"No honor among thieves," O'Davis said. "Musta planned on killin' the Americans all along, then hijackin' the boat with the money."

"Must have," I said. I felt the old depression that always sweeps over me in a wave after I have contributed to the unreasonable loss of someone's life.

I studied the bodies of the three Rastafarians. Born into poverty in some Jamaican shithole, what chance did any of them really have? And who wouldn't have grabbed at the first religion that promised them escape—escape and the emotional relief of drugs?

They had been victims. My victims. Life's victims.

Still, there must come a time when excuses are of little consequence; a time when every man must stand accountable for the sum total of self. And I am not talking about the Christian Judgment Day, either. No matter what a man's past, no matter how desperate the exigencies of his life, there must arrive a day when blame or praise sits squarely upon his own shoulders.

If the moral codes of a society are to survive, the actions of an adult life cannot be forgiven or excused by the difficulties of childhood.

These three had been victims. Victims of poverty, victims of a pitiful youth, and, in the end, victims of their own greed and hatred.

They would have murdered the Irishman and myself without flinching—just as they had murdered the two American drug runners.

But still I felt the wave of depression. The Rastafarian who had been driven through the window by the Thompson's .45 slugs lay at an odd angle, as if his bones were made of rubber. The pool of blood from the Rastafarian O'Davis had shot was beginning to thicken. There was a purple clot forming on the neck of the third Jamaican beneath the matted beard.

It all seemed such a waste; such a damnable waste.

O'Davis stood silently beside me. He cleared his throat. "I could use a drink, Yank."

"I might try some of that Irish whiskey myself."

From outside came the muted roar of an outboard starting. It was Onard Cribbs, trying to get away in the powerboat.

Westy caught my eyes. "I get the distinct impression, brother MacMorgan, that Cribbs is responsible fer this whole bloody business."

"Yeah," I said, "He was playing one side against the other."

The Irishman ejected one clip from his Thompson submachine gun and jammed in a fresh one. "I think we ought ta have a talk with the man."

"We can still catch him?"

"I've got the fastest boat on the island, re-member?" The Irishman's smile was not a pretty thing to see. "Grand Cayman is a civil place, an' the authorities will not be likin' this slaughter. If someone is to get a chewin' out, I'd prefer it be Cribbs."

"Fine," I said. "Try not to fall too far behind."

"Hah!" O'Davis snorted. "I'll be startin' the boat by the time the likes o' you hits the water!"

In truth, we got to his ratty cruiser at the same time. We sprinted across the back lawn through the humid March darkness to the bluff above the sea.

The speedboat was a pale wake line searching for an exit through the reef.

"Doesn't know the water, our Jamaican friend!" O'Davis yelled. "If he doesn't find the cut, we'll have 'im sure."

We clattered down the steps we had es-chewed earlier, then made our way along the rocky shore to the coconut palms which hid our gear. We didn't waste time trying to be quiet and careful now. We charged into the water and struck out for the boat, holding the submachine guns high.

Onard Cribbs did find the cut. Over my shoul-der, I saw the skiff glimmering in the moonlight as it knifed through the breakers at the seaward edge of the reef. I expected him to cut east toward North Sound. But he didn't. Instead, he seemed to be headed west toward open sea.

I remembered the pickup boat. It was supposed to belong to the dead drug runner, Morro. But maybe Cribbs was in deeper than even Morro knew.

Little bells began going off in my head.

It would have to be a big oceangoing boat, a diesel-powered vessel with a hell of a range, to carry drugs from Grand Cayman to point X, because Grand Cayman is in the middle of nowhere.

The kidnappers had to be counting on such a vessel. By phone they had demanded an air rendezvous with a ship at sea. And maybe that's why a careful land search of the island hadn't produced young Thomas James—because they already had him sequestered aboard.

When we finally climbed onto the cruiser and I had hauled anchor, I told O'Davis what I was thinking.

He nodded shortly. "Could be, Yank. Could be. An' it's all the more reason to have a talk with Mr. Cribbs."

The Irishman gunned the boat, jumping her onto plane. The sea wind had freshened with midnight, and we were pounding right into the greasy, moon-slick swells. While O'Davis fought with the wheel, I switched on the VHF and tried to raise Cayman police. And just when I was about to give up, a voice came back: "Vessel calling, this is Grand Cayman."

I gave them an eyeball position, told them we were in pursuit, and asked for assistance. There was a long wait. I could imagine the dispatcher at his desk in Georgetown making phone calls, waking his superiors.

Finally, there was this: "Power vessel *Rogue*, this is Grand Cayman. We will be sending assistance by sea and air. But there will be about an hour before they reach your position. We still have to wake the helicopter pilot."

O'Davis was chuckling to himself as I signed off. "Hah! Sleepy little island, Grand Cayman!"

"Yeah, but an hour . . ."

"Oh, we'll be lucky if it only takes 'em an hour, Yank. That's what I love about livin' here. Don't have yer perverted American sense of time!"

We used the Q-beam to find the cut this time. The surf was a churning, frozen haze in the distance. Cribbs was too far away for the light to reflect off his hull.

We crashed through the first breakers into the standing chop that marked the cut, then twisted through to open sea.

I switched off the light and returned to the cabin. O'Davis handed me the binoculars. They made the stars burn fiercely on the horizon and gave me a better look at the powerboat in the distance.

"He's about a quarter mile ahead of us—a few points to starboard."

"Aye, I see 'im now!"

I kept a close eye on Cribbs through the binoculars. He seemed to know where he wanted to go—because only a fool or someone with a destination would head for open sea in a small boat. I noticed something else, too:

"He's pulling away from us," I said.

"What?"

"I thought you said this was the fastest boat on the island, O'Davis."

"It is!"

"Than why are we losing ground?"

The Irishman gave me an indignant look, then patted the Morse controls of the boat lovingly. "Don't ya be lettin' me down now, darlin'. Give us jest a touch more petrol, eh?" Using his weight, he tried to mash the throttles even farther forward. But his *Rogue* was giving us all she had. We went crashing through the swells at a rolling forty miles an hour.

Finally convinced, O'Davis turned to me meekly.

"That bloody speedboat must not be from Grand Cayman."

"Oh, yeah—that explains it."

"I'm afraid it gives rise to a new list of problems, Yank."

"Should I act surprised? Cribbs is going to beat us to the mother ship. If we try to get close enough to board, they'll shoot us before we get out of the cabin—if they don't shoot and sink us before. The Cayman police are coming like the cavalry, by sea and air. If the kid is aboard, they'll kill him at the first sound of a chopper." I paused. "Does that pretty much sum things up?"

"It does, it does," he said lamely. "Any ideas?"

"We could turn back now and call off the police."

"Ah," he said, "that's what a wise man would do. Yes indeed, a wise man would certainly turn back now."

"Of course, that would give them time to get into international or even Cuban waters. If they have the kid, they'll still be holding all the cards."

"But a wise man would turn back," the Irishman repeated sagely.

"I notice you're still holding course."

O'Davis panned his head around the cabin

theatrically. "Ya know, 'tis a strang thing, Yank—but I do na see a wise man aboard."

"Westy, sometimes you're one extraordinary, foolhardy Irishman."

He smiled. "An' sometimes, Mr. Dusky Mac-Morgan, you are an extraordinary judge of character."

13

The mother ship was ghostly in the distance, pale in the moonglow. There were no lights anywhere. The windows of the wheelhouse were a sheen of silver.

The men aboard were obviously being careful. They didn't want to be seen. I watched the ship through the binoculars. The sea had no bottom here, so they drifted, rolling in the ocean's swell.

It was a commercial trawler, the wheelhouse mounted far forward with a huge expanse of stern deck for working the trawl nets. The hull was white with black trim. It flew no flag from the triangle of masthead.

"Is Cribbs there yet?"

"Just pulling alongside. A couple guys from the trawler are out on the deck trying to help him aboard."

"Think they know we're followin', Dusky?"

"They have to know. You know how sound travels over water."

"Aye. An' they'll be keepin' a close eye on this boat." He backed off on the throttles. Our own wake lifted our stern, then dropped us back into the trough. The trawler was about a half mile dead ahead. "Any ideas, Yank?"

"You may have just given me one."

"Very smart of me—what is it?"

"They'll be keeping an eye on this boat."

"Aye—the boat an' us too. I do na think we kin go swimmin' up to their vessel without bein' aerated by their blinkin' guns."

"We can if we do it right. Do you have a fuel-line shutoff valve?"

"Aye—they're required. You know that."

"Than get this boat back on plane and put us directly astern of the trawler. Maybe a quarter mile off. And just hope those Thompsons of yours can stand a little more salt water."

As we banged along closer to the trawler, a big marine searchlight blinked on above the cabin. They swept it along behind us, then held us in the beam.

"Bloody rude of 'em," the Irishman yelled, shielding his eyes.

"I don't think they're very nice people."

"Need some manners, is all! An' it's me great hope that it's meself who teaches 'em!"

When we were well astern of the trawler, I had O'Davis drop us back to idle. They held the searchlight on us, but from that distance—even with binoculars—they wouldn't be able to see what we were doing. While the Irishman got our gear ready, I pulled off the engine-compartment hatch. The shutoff valve on the fuel line had a common case of saltwater corrosion. It took me a while to bust it free. When I had it working, I summoned the Irishman.

"Point us away from the trawler. Get us up on plane. I need to see how long the engine will run with the fuel valve shut."

"An' suddenly, I see what ya have planned, brother MacMorgan."

"Well?"

"It may work. But I hate ta see me boat get shot up so."

"Better it than us."

"No argument there, mate."

"Just run at your most economical speed—if there's such a thing on this gas hog."

"Hog, is it? Ya jest keep an eye on that fancy watch of yers!"

When we were running evenly into the swell, I twisted the valve and marked the time on the

luminescent dial, of my Rolex. After a minute
and a half, the engine began to sputter. Then
it died.

"Will it give us enough time, Yank?"

"A minute and forty-three seconds," I yelled
back. "It'll be close. But we don't have much
choice." I primed the engine, opened the valve,
then pulled on fins, mask, and snorkel. O'Davis
handed me the Thompson. I said, "We'd better
hurry. Right now they're deciding if they should
make a run for it. Let's catch them while they're
still thinking."

O'Davis started his *Rogue* on the third try,
then nosed us around, putting the bow just off
the stern of the big trawler. I had to remind him
to keep the RPM down. The fuel was flowing
freely now, but once I shut it off I didn't want
any change of speed to make them suspicious.

My plan was simple. We would go charging
right at them. I was counting on them to open
fire. Then O'Davis would veer away from the
trawler when I flipped off the fuel valve. Their
fire would explain our sudden change of course.
When we were as close as possible to the
trawler, the Irishman and I would tumble unseen into the water. Their eyes, very naturally,
would follow the boat as it continued on its
course. The boat would run for almost two minutes on the fuel in the line. Then it would stop.

They might think we were hit. Or they might think we had stopped to regroup. Whatever they thought, they wouldn't be expecting us to slip up over the stern.

We were about four hundred yards off, heading straight for their stern, when the windshield exploded. Wood began splintering on the deck. Their weapons were brief darts of flame in the distance.

"So far so good, Yank—if the buggers don't kill us before we get there."

O'Davis held fast to our course, running toward them like a kamikaze pilot. They must have thought we were crazy. And maybe we were.

Staying low, I ducked down into the engine hatch.

"Ready, Westy?"

"An Irishman's born ready!"

We were about seventy-five yards from the trawler when I jammed the fuel valve off—but it seemed one hell of a lot closer. The drug runners suffered no shortage of automatic firepower. They were working us over with about a half-dozen light weapons that sounded like M-16s. The Irishman's *Rogue* was being carved into splinters.

"Hope yer right about them concentratin' on the boat, MacMorgan!"

"Just in case—it's been interesting knowing you, O'Davis."

"Been a real treat fer me too, ya big ugly brute!"

The Irishman threw the wheel half to starboard and lashed it at my order. And when the stern swung, we let the momentum throw us off the starboard side—the side away from the trawler.

I didn't carry a big breath of air with me. I wanted to sink. And I did. I wanted to stay down just as long as I could. And I had told O'Davis to do the same. They would be watching the cruiser, following it with their guns.

I hoped.

From ten feet down, the surface of the sea was moon-bright, stars slightly out of focus. I felt something brush the back of me and realized it was the Irishman swimming toward the top. I grabbed his arm and held him. When his squirming told me he needed air, I drifted upward with him.

The searchlight aboard the trawler still held the little white cruiser in its beam. It was angling away from us at a respectable twenty knots. They had brought up more firepower, emptying round after round into the wooden hull.

There was no time to waste. Taking care not to splash with our fins, we set out for the trawler as fast as we could possibly go. We lifted and fell with every swell. Stars threw trembling paths before us. The sound of men yelling pierced the staccato gunfire.

As long as they didn't start engines and run for it, and as long as the salt water didn't render the old Thompsons useless, we were in good shape.

We were only about twenty yards from the stern of the trawler when we heard the *Rogue*'s engines sputter and then die. Someone yelled something, and then the gunfire stopped, too.

I could hear the metallic fluttering of a halyard against the masthead and the wash of waves against the hull of the trawler. Their voices were clear now. More Jamaican voices.

"What you figure they doin', mon?"

"Goddamn if I know!"

"They dead, mon. Nobody live through that shit."

The fourth voice I recognized. It was Cribbs. He couldn't hide the fear. "Don' be so sure, mon. Goddamn cops. Shot the shit outta Benji and Marley an' that other nigger."

"Who you callin' nigger, nigger! You're the crazy fool who led them cops out here!"

"Gotta get them engines started, mon. Gotta get the hell away from Georgetown!"

"You don' hear good, nigger? I tell you, mon,

the engine she busted. Woody down there work-in' on her now. We leave Georgetown—soon as them rusty bastards get fixed.''

"Got to think o' somethin', mon,'' Onard Cribbs insisted. "Killin' two Yankee drug run-ners one thing, mon. Killin' them two cops on tha' boat som'pin' else. Maybe I'm gonna get back on tha' speedboat—''

"The hell you say, mon. Anybody use that speedboat, we use it! You the crazy one who brung the cops back here.''

"Didn' know, mon. Hear me, I didn' know! Yankee drug runners fall for it too easy. They musta been in on it.''

"Shit, mon, you just stupid, that what you are!''

They argued on and on. The Jamaican drug runners were finding that their sweet scheme had suddenly gone very damn sour indeed. They had somehow tricked the two Americans into believing the mother ship and the heroin suppliers were manned by two separate fac-tions. All the Americans had done was finance the whole operation—and their own deaths.

I listened closely, hoping they would make some mention of the kidnapped boy.

But they never did.

The transom of the trawler loomed high above

us. In large block letters the name on the stern read, "*Hotcake*—Kingston, Jamaica."

The Irishman and I found handholds on the exhaust pipes which protruded from the water-line. The boat heaved and rolled in the wash of sea. It stank of oil and rotten fish. O'Davis motioned for me to lean close, and he whispered in my ear, "I'm gettin' the feelin' they don't know nothin' about the James lad."

"Yeah. Me too. Maybe we'd better just wait for the Cayman police to get here."

"It's still gonna be messy, Yank. Very messy. They think they've killed us. Jammed inta a bit of a corner, they are. I suspect they'll try to stand and fight it out."

I nodded and said nothing, knowing O'Davis was right. Whatever happened, we would be right in the middle. I felt disgusted with myself. This was becoming more and more of a scorched-earth mission. Still, if they had the boy, I had chosen the only reasonable plan of action. And now we would have to live with it. Or die with it.

"It was my idea," I whispered. "No sense in letting your Cayman police force drop into an ambush. We'd better get them softened up. I'll go first."

"Thought ye would never offer," the Irishman said and grinned.

There was a coil of line hanging down from the port cleat. I slipped my fins off and belted them to the small of my back. With the Thompson slung over my shoulder, I pulled myself up to the stern rail and peered over. Five men clustered on the bow point beneath the spotlight, still watching O'Davis' cruiser in the distance. I could see the glare of Onard Cribbs' shaved head.

Closer to me, on the stern deck, I could hear a voice. The engine hatch was open. Someone was below, cursing softly to himself. It was Woodie, the guy working on the diesels. I pulled the Randall knife from its scabbard and climbed onto the deck, hiding myself as best I could behind the draping nets. When I was sure the other men were still busy with their arguing, I moved across the expanse of deck. The engine hold was brightly lighted with a mechanic's lamp. A wooden ladder with five rungs ended in an oily bilge slick. The Jamaican had his back to me, crouched over one of the fuel pumps. He was a small wiry man with hair in Rastafarian braids. He was trying to piece the fuel pump back together. I poised over the hold, took a deep breath, then dropped down on top of him, cracking him as hard as I could on the nape of the neck with my elbow.

He never knew what hit him. He collapsed

with a low-pitched *whoof* and fell still upon the engine.

I checked the side of his neck with two fingers. The jugular was still pumping blood, strong and steady. There was electrician's tape in the tool box. I taped his hands, legs, and mouth, then climbed back to the transom and summoned the Irishman.

Just as O'Davis got over the transom, one of the Jamaicans decided to come aft to check and see how Woodie was doing. We dove for cover behind nets on opposite sides of the deck. The Jamaican stood scratching his head, perplexed to find the engine hatch closed. Then, from the pile of net which hid the Irishman, came a strange warbling whistle. The Jamaican heard it. He hesitated for a moment, then decided to investigate.

That's just what O'Davis wanted him to do.

When the Jamaican poked his head around the net, O'Davis was waiting and ready. I could see them both clearly. The Jamaican's face described bewilderment and then alarm.

But he never got a chance to call out. The Irishman had his fist drawn back, like a pitcher ready to release a fast ball. He hit him square on the point of beard which hid his chin. The Jamaican backpedaled across the deck mechanically, already knocked cold.

I caught him before he fell.

"Things will be gettin' tougher now, Yank," O'Davis whispered, flexing the knuckles of his right hand.

"There are five more up there. At least five. Could be somebody down in the cabin, but I doubt it."

"If we take 'em by surprise, we might not have ta fire a shot."

"I'm all for that."

Westy opened the engine hatch, and I lifted the dead weight of the second Jamaican into the hold. I used the rest of the electrician's tape to gag and bind him.

O'Davis was standing at the bulkhead of the wheelhouse, submachine gun ready, watching the other Jamaicans. Their arguing had given way to plain fear. And they were nervous. Very nervous.

"What the hell takin' daht Woodie so long?"

"Don' know, mon. Sent Switch ta check on him. Hey dah, Switch! What goin' on back dah, mon?"

And that's when O'Davis made the mistake of trying to imitate the Rastafarian he had coldcocked.

But it was a chance he had to take. We needed just a little more time to position ourselves.

"Engine doin' fine, mon!" O'Davis called back in a muted voice.

Unfortunately it sounded like just what it was: an Irishman doing a bad impression of a Jamaican. It didn't fool anyone—least of all the five men waiting on the bow of the trawler. They exchanged knowing glances, then came charging toward the stern, their M-16s vectoring.

14

For a few seconds, it was like one very, very deadly game of tag.

They came running down the starboard side of the wheelhouse while we hustled forward along the port side. They weren't the least bit reluctant to fire. Slugs exploded into the deck behind us like dogs at our heels.

There was no doubt what they would do when they found the stern deck empty: split up and surround the wheelhouse. And we couldn't afford to let them succeed, because, if they got us in a cross fire we were both dead.

In midstride, I put one foot on the port railing and threw myself up on top of the cabin, I heard the Irishman land heavily behind me.

"You take the stern; I'll cover the bow!"

"Thanks!"

When two of the Jamaicans came sliding around the corner, I let them have it.

Thankfully, the old Thompson still worked. Shell casings clattered onto the fiberglass roof as I held the trigger down, sweeping a spray of .45 caliber slugs across them, the sound of the submachine gun ringing in my ears, the wooden handgrip wet beneath my palm.

The two of them jolted back across the deck as if they were being electrocuted. Their weapons flew from their hands, and their eyes showed glazed surprise.

One of them tumbled backward over the railing, splashing into the moon-soft water.

The other collapsed spread-eagled upon a coil of anchor line, limp as a rag doll, his eyes showing neither surprise nor wonder now.

They were as empty as all death. . . .

The Irishman had yet to fire a shot. He stretched out in prone position behind an orange life raft with a woven rope bottom. The searchlight was still on, throwing a smoky beam across the turquoise water.

Using both hands, I swung the lamp around, illuminating the stern deck in stark white light.

The other three Jamaicans weren't quite as gung-ho now. They were hiding somewhere beneath us in the cabin or wheelhouse, waiting for us to make the next move.

And my swinging the spotlight around had been move enough. It was a stupid thing for me to do. It told them where we were. At first, I didn't know where the shots were coming from. But then an ellipse of explosions perforated the roof planking.

They were shooting *up* at us. For them, it was a random but deadly ace in the hole. We had nowhere to go; no flybridge on which to take refuge. And if we tried to jump down to the deck, the Jamaicans would sure as hell have the windows covered, ready and waiting.

"Makes a fella want ta sprout wings!" the Irishman whispered anxiously.

All three automatics opened up this time, crisscrossing the wheelhouse roof with splinters. O'Davis had jumped to his feet, toeing the edge of the overhang, clinging gingerly to the masthead bracing which supported the white anchorage light and radio antennas. Holding the Thompson in one hand, he opened up with a burst of his own.

The return fire was heavy—and concentrated in his area.

"Don't try that again!" I whispered hoarsely. They had far too much room to hide below. An exchange of fire on our part was insanity.

"Bloody stupid of me," the Irishman mumbled, swearing at himself. "But what in the hell are we gonna do, Yank?"

The Jamaicans began a methodical sweep of the roof area with their M-16s.

It was the only thing that saved us. If they had continued their random fire, we would have stepped into it. Sooner or later, they would have killed us.

But the orderly sweep pattern gave us time to anticipate—and move.

And just enough time for me to come up with a plan.

Not much of a plan.

But it was all we had.

I grabbed the Irishman's arm as we cake-walked forward atop the wheelhouse, staying ahead of the fire pattern. "Get ready to jump," I said into his ear.

"Onto th' deck?"

"No—the water. Gotta go headfirst. And deep. Swim clear under the boat and come up on the other side."

"I'm not about ta leave ya up here by yer-self—"

"Just do it. I'll be right behind."

O'Davis didn't hesitate. At the next burst of fire, he threw himself headlong toward the dark sea. And at the same moment, I rolled across the deck and heaved the little life raft after him.

Below, all they would see were two fleeting

shapes passing the cabin windows. And they would hear two distinct splashes.

If we had any luck left at all, they would think we had both dived into the water.

I crouched on the planking of the wheelhouse waiting. The firing stopped abruptly.

"They're swimmin' for it, mon!"

"That good!"

"Get out there an' kill 'em. Get!"

The three of them came charging out the cabin door onto the deck. I expected them to come out shooting, but they didn't. They were a little smarter than I had given them credit for. They fanned out along the starboard railing, where O'Davis had jumped. It didn't take them long to see it.

"Goddamn life raft, mon!"

"What the hell . . ."

"Hold it!" I pressed myself against the top of the wheelhouse, submachine gun focused on the man in the middle—Onard Cribbs. I wanted to take them alive. There was still an outside chance they might know something about the kidnapped boy. And even if they didn't, there had already been too much killing. There's an old saying: Every living thing killed deadens the killer a little more. . . .

And I had already had more than my share of killing. There is an ever increasing number of

the sickies: men and women who enjoy the
seeping life force, the fluttering eyes, and the
gray gray cold of death. Those are the ones with
snakes burrowed in their brains. The elite few
become the hired hit men—people who revel in
the crimson kiss. But most just wind up in pad-
ded cells after climbing their own tragic bell
towers.

And I find only horror in those bell-tower
steps.

"Hold your weapons out over the water. Move!"

Cribbs and the other Jamaican didn't hesitate.
They did as told. But the third had to play the
hero. He was a hugely fat man with a sweaty
football of a head. I knew what he was going to
do before he tried it. He tensed, crouched, then
whirled around, already firing.

One of the slugs hit the spotlight. It exploded
in a spray of smoke and glass. I felt something
sting my face; felt the hot stream of blood. His
move triggered Cribbs and the other Rastafarian. They both dove to the deck, rolled, and
opened up with their M-16s. With the searchlight out, they could not see me plainly.

It saved my life.

I cut the fat Jamaican down with a short burst,
then held the trigger of the Thompson as I
sprayed Cribbs and the third Rastafarian. It's a
sickening sound, the pumpkin-thud of low-

speed .45 slugs entering a body. The fat man writhed momentarily on the deck, then lay still. Cribbs moaned out pitifully.

"You kill me, mon! You goddamn kill me. . . ."

I jumped down on the deck. Behind me, I could hear O'Davis pulling himself up over the stern. His beard was dripping; his face was stained with an oval of black from his face mask.

"Thought ya said you were gonna jump, Yank."

"I lied."

"Aye." And then he smiled; a smile that implied appreciation, not humor. "An' ye saved me life, I'm thinkin'."

"Both of our lives. But I owed you one, remember?"

"Three," he corrected quickly. "I've saved yers three times."

"And if we're both real lucky, I'll never get a chance to repay the other two."

I knelt beside Cribbs. His chest and shoulder were a spongy line of blood. But he was still alive. Beneath his shaved head, his eyes were two black orbs.

"You kill me . . . bastard . . ."

"That's right, Cribbs. You're dying."

"All busted up inside, mon."

"A chopper's on its way. If you can hang on, we'll get you to a hospital."

His breath was coming in labored gasps now. He lay still, eyes burrowing into me. I said, "Cribbs—the boy. Where's the boy?"

His eyes didn't change. And he said nothing.

"Cribbs, you're dying. If you know where the boy is, don't let him die, too!"

His lips pursed as if to say something. He tilted his head back, heaved, then lay perfectly still, eyes still open, but empty.

He had died trying to spit in my face. . . .

By the time the helicopter arrived, O'Davis and I had helped the two bound Rastafarians out of the engine compartment. They were still groggy. We sat them on the deck and tried to make them talk.

They looked bewildered when I asked them about the kidnapping of Thomas James.

"Don' know nothin', mon. We jest work on this boat."

They kept staring at the corpses strewn around the deck.

"We're not going to kill you," I insisted. "If you help us, we'll help you. The boy—where is he?"

"Don' know nothin' 'bout no boy. Just work on this boat."

The helicopter came hovering down beside the trawler, red flight lights popping, the roar

deafening. O'Davis' adviser from Government
House was in the cramped third seat. The sleek
powerboat was still tethered alongside the
trawler. The Irishman went over to the chopper
while I stayed with the prisoners.

His English adviser was not pleased. He pre-
ceded the Irishman, climbing over the stern. The
disdain was easy to read as he surveyed the
deck. He was a thin man, medium height, with
wire-rim glasses that somehow made him look
older than his fifty-odd years. I remembered his
name only as Henderson.

He gave me a cursory look, then ignored me
during the rest of the conversation.

"Is this how you win your medals, Commander O'Davis—wholesale slaughter?"

"An' I suppose we shoulda jest sat back while
they killed us."

"I daresay that was one option," he said in a
clipped tone. "Did you stop to consider that this
might be a matter better handled by the police?"

"We thought they might have the boy—sahr."

"But they don't?"

"No," the Irishman said glumly.

"Georgetown police had a report of gunfire
coming from the Canadian's estate. They inves-
tigated. They found a number of bodies." He
looked at O'Davis sharply. "Is it your intent to

eliminate everyone on Grand Cayman until chance brings the kidnappers under your fire?"

"My intent—*sahr*—is ta find th' lad an' return him safely to his parents. These men are heroin smugglers. Two of the bodies th' police found at the Canadian's estate died by their hand. They woulda killed us—or yerself—jest as gladly. We thought they might know somethin' about the lad. We followed them."

"So I see."

O'Davis was building up a fine head of Irish anger. "An' one more thing—*sahr*. If ye have any more complaints about me work, please direct them to headquarters in London. An' if ye like, demand they replace one of us. I'm sure ya'd enjoy spendin' spring in yer beloved England."

We waited just long enough for the police cruisers to arrive. When they took charge of the trawler and the two prisoners, we had one of their men ferry us back to the Irishman's cruiser. The cabin had been shot to hell, but the engines worked fine—once I remembered to open the fuel valve.

O'Davis was oddly silent as he stood at the wheel, the boat jumping full-bore through the moon-slick swells toward Grand Cayman's North Sound.

"He got to you, didn't he?" I said softly, standing beside him in the damaged cabin.

"Aye, he did," he said bitterly. "It's a victory fer him. He's been at me throat ever since he took the post more than a year ago."

I had left a tin of Copenhagen on the console. I opened it, took a big pinch for myself, then handed it to the Irishman. "He didn't get to you. The killing did."

He nodded slowly. "Yer right, Yank. Yer right."

"We had no choice."

He shrugged his shoulders sadly.

I sighed. It was a pretty night: bright moon and frozen stars against a black tropical sky. A meteor flared through the darkness and faded. I said, "Don't suppose you have a cooler full of beer aboard this wreck of yours?"

He smiled for the first time. "No—but I have a pint of fine Irish whiskey."

"Only a pint?"

"Don't worry, Yank. I'll leave a swaller fer you."

15

By the time we got back to the mooring in North Sound, it was nearly four A.M.

In the dark mass of shore, birds were beginning to make their morning sounds.

A rooster crowed. Trees began to move in a freshening dawn wind.

O'Davis had decided to leave his boat at Bota Bano and bring it around to Gun Bay Village after getting a few hours of sleep. We both felt the unspoken tension: time. We didn't have much more time. Only one and a half days to save a boy we had never met.

But the whiskey had relaxed him. And me too. Normally, I drink only beer. But the whiskey had filled me with a fine warm glow against the cold breath of the previous evening.

We climbed up the bank through the trees past the sleeping island homes.

O'Davis drove. Before we had left the police boat, he had told the officer in charge about our suspicions concerning Sir Conan James. Unlike Henderson from Government House, the police treated O'Davis with open deference; respect bordering on awe. They said our information would be added to the file on the late Cynthia Rothchild, and that they would put a discreet tail on Sir Conan.

So we had no immediate work for the morning. Only sleep.

It was a very early Sunday morning on Grand Cayman. Streets were deserted, houses and condos along Seven Mile Beach dark. Even the sea seemed to be resting; the moon was low on the westward horizon now, adding a pearly luminescence to the exhalations of coral sea.

O'Davis steered the Fiat attentively, lights funneling through the early-morning darkness.

He said, "Mornin's like this, brother MacMorgan, that a man needs a good woman ta share his bed."

"Have you turned mind reader?"

He chuckled shortly. "Ye've got a mind easy ta read, Yank. Didna ya mention that yer lady lives along here somewhere?"

"About a half mile on toward Georgetown. Are you offering to drop me?"

"Aye. I am." He looked at me, his face dimly seen in the glow of dashboard lights. "I know what yer thinkin'. Yer thinkin' I'm feelin' a bit o' depression an' that ye might be better stayin' with me fer the company." He was silent for a moment. "I appreciate the concern, but I'm no stranger ta the black mood. And yer not either, I'm thinkin'. Comes with our line of work—and a bloody line o' work it is at times, eh?"

"Yeah. Yeah, it is."

"Killin' makes ya look in the mirror an' see the skull beneath yer own skin. Ya jest got ta give it time; let it seep outta ya like mist from a bog." He slapped me affectionately on the shoulder. "So I'll be fine, Yank. Don't be worryin' about me. I'll go on back ta me wee cottage by the sea, drink a bottle o' stout, and sag into me bed—jealous of the bed you'll be sharin'," he added with a laugh.

At Sea Mist Apartments, the colored lights on the palm trees still made it look like some scene from a tropical hell. I waved good-bye to the Irishman, slammed the door of the Fiat, and walked quietly through the darkness along the parking lot.

I heard the odd mannish sobbing just before I reached the stairs to Diacona Ebanks' apartment. In the quiet morning dusk, the sound seemed to come from all sides. It took me a long moment to pinpoint it.

I ducked in behind one of the parked cars and peered around. It came from a sleek new Mercedes. The door was open and the courtesy light showed a man with dark hair slumped over the steering wheel, crying into his hands.

It was the sort of anguished male sobbing that made hair on the nape of the neck stand; a crying that triggered all the prehistoric instincts.

It was Sir Conan James.

I had been dazed with need of sleep before, but now I was wide awake. All the little alarms were going off, and I found my breath coming soft and shallow, adrenaline pumping through my body.

Sir Conan was crying; the suspected sadist in tears.

Why?

My eyes panned quickly up the side of the apartment building. Dia's lights were on—the only lights in the whole building. I noticed my hands were suddenly shaking. If he had murdered Cynthia Rothchild, the woman who had spurned him, maybe Dia had become number two in the chain.

Suddenly, Sir Conan slammed the door of the car, punched it into gear, and screeched out of the parking lot.

Blood was pounding loud in my ears. I took the steps three at a time. There was a rustling in the bushes. I paid no attention. At her door, I banged with full fist. Again and again and—

"Dusky!"

She stood trembling in the angle of light, clutching the bathrobe around her neck. Her eyes were puffy, red from crying.

"My God, Dusky, what's happened to you?"

I took her in my arms and swung her around, kicking the door closed behind. In the drama of the moment I learned how much I had come to care for this wild island girl with the lilting Cayman accent. She clung to me tightly, her fingers pulling my face against her wet cheek.

She was crying and laughing at the same time. "Dusky, your head—what happened to your head?"

And I suddenly realized what a sight I must have been—my wounds from the exploding searchlight untended, blood crusted in sun-bleached hair.

So, when I released her, I kissed her soft lips once, then sat her down on the couch beside me.

"I had a little accident. Nothing major."

"Let me get an astringent and some bandages—"

"That can wait. I saw Sir Conan outside."

She shook her head wearily and sighed. Her

bathrobe was a burnt orange, and it brought out the subtle shades of soft smoke-brown hair and brown island eyes. "He was here," she said softly.

"You let him in?"

"No!" And then, more controlled: "No, you told me not to. I wouldn't have anyway." She rubbed an open palm across her forehead, her distress plain to see. "Dusky," she said, "Jimmy's gone mad! Totally and completely mad. His face, his eyes—they were so awful to see. Like a wild man. His pounding was waking up everybody, so I finally had to crack the door with the lock chain on."

"What did he say?"

"He wanted in. He begged me. He . . ." She spasmed, gasped, then broke down, sobbing. I pulled her head against my chest, stroking her soft hair. When she was better under control, I got up and rummaged through the cupboards until I found a bottle of B&B liqueur. I poured a healthy ration in a tumbler, then took it to her.

"Drink this."

Like a little girl, she wiped nose and eyes with a small fist and took the drink obediently.

"Feel better?"

She nodded. "God, how awful I must look."

"You look fine."

She finished the liqueur in a long swallow.

"It's just that it was so hard turning him away when I had cared so much for him."

"I know."

"But he was like a wild man, Dusky. Not mean like the night you saw him—he was more . . . pathetic. Like a lost little lad without a friend."

"Did he threaten you?"

She thought, shaking her head. "No. I don't think so. He said so much, so fast. Rather incoherent things. Wild things. He was very upset about the kidnapping of his son. He kept . . . blaming himself. He said there was blood on his hands. Isn't that awful?"

"Yes," I said. "Yes, it is."

She looked at me and hesitated. "You were looking for his son tonight, weren't you? That's how you got those cuts."

"Yes."

"Did you find him? I so hope you did. . . ."

"No."

She touched my face gently with her fingertips. "Something bad happened to you tonight. I can see it in your eyes."

"Business. That's all. It's nothing for you to worry about."

"Such a considerate liar you are." She took my head in her palms and pulled my lips to hers. It was a gentle kiss, like a salve, full of affection. "You're exhausted, aren't you?"

"Yes."

"I can see that in your eyes, too."

"My eyes are very talkative tonight."

"And you're not."

"Sometimes there's nothing to say." I traced her lips with my index finger. "Sometimes silence among two people means more than talk."

She took my finger in her small hand and squeezed it. Her face was very, very close to mine, the tropical generations of her forebears beautiful to see in the mahogany skin.

"I have something to say."

"What's that?"

She tilted her head and kissed me gently. "I . . . love you, Dusky MacMorgan." She drew her head back and smiled. "There. I said it. I promised myself I would after the last time you left. I had this awful feeling I would never see you again."

"You're just trying to turn my pretty head."

She slapped at me. "Can't you be serious?"

"I thought you didn't like that word—love."

"You've changed my mind."

"In only two days?"

"You're very very persuasive." She turned suddenly away from me. "And now that I've said it, I feel . . ."

"Vulnerable?"

"Yes. How did you know?"

How did I know? Because my failure to voice my own love for her could only leave her feeling uncertain. I had not played my roll; had not spoken my part: "I love you." "Yes, and I love *you*." That's the way it's supposed to go. But long ago, in a distant lifetime, I had lost the one all-encompassing love of my life. And now the words wouldn't come for me; not for the beautiful Diacona Ebanks or for anyone else. Maybe I was feeling sorry for myself. Or punishing myself. Guilt lingers in the wake of any great loss. Yes, I did love this lady in my own way, as much as I could love any woman after only two days. There can be little doubt that there are both negative and positive chemistries between two people. And our interest in each other was both mutual and immediate—from our first meeting on the plane. And my feelings for her had increased tenfold since.

"I know you feel vulnerable because that's the way I feel when I'm around you."

"Oh . . ." she said softly, gratefully, "that's such a nice way to put it." She buried her face on my chest, kissing my neck, hands sliding up and down my sides. "Hey—your sweater's wet."

"Decided it was a nice night for a swim."

"And your pants, too."

"Is this a survey?"

"I've just got busy hands, that's all. And my hands also say that you're not as exhausted as you pretend to be."

"What demands you make on an old man."

"I didn't hear that—the sound of that awful zipper blocked out everything. Where did you get these pants, anyway? A yard sale?"

"They're lucky. Don't knock my lucky knickers."

"So that's what they are?" She dropped down to her knees, off the couch, pulling at the pants. "And you can't afford underwear, either?"

"I'm very poor."

Her face was flushed brighter than with the tears. "You don't look so impoverished from this angle."

"Where do you get all your energy?"

"It's all that flying. The air's better up there."

She touched her tongue to the inside of my knee, tracing the line of my inner thigh. I bent over her, nose buried in her hair, and found the cord which held the robe. It came undone with a tug. I cupped her heavy breasts in my hands while her face and tongue vectored upward. Finally, when I could stand it no more, I stood her up and stripped the robe off her shoulders. Her eyes were hazed, voice thick.

"Please, Dusky, please . . . yes . . . let's forget this awful night. . . ."

Let's forget this awful night.

So I lifted the lady into my arms, my mouth finding hers, and carried her toward the darkened bedroom and that ultimate release of all cares, all worries . . . and all memories. Something had been added to our lovemaking; something sweet and sad. The frenzy of our first coupling was replaced by something new . . . gentleness, affection . . . and maybe a mutual haven of understanding that, if the world can wound, love can heal.

And when we were spent, when the memories and the fears had been released in the torrent of climax, she lay with her head cradled on my chest, hand tiny on my chest. Outside, the Cayman dawn was copper-colored, streaked with blue. Through the thin walls of the apartment came the sounds of toilets flushing and blaring wake-up radios; people readying for the new day. But no amount of daylight or noise could have kept either of us from sleep. And just before I drifted off, I heard her Cayman voice like a folk song, saying, "I love you Dusky. . . ." And I heard another voice, this one deeper, familiar, but still a stranger: "And I love you too, Dia. Very much. . . ."

16

I woke to a nightmare.

The whole time, I kept thinking: *This has to be a dream. This can't be real.*

I kept wanting to pinch myself; kept wanting to make it all go away and disappear forever and ever.

But it was no dream.

There was the sound of a lightbulb popping. And then another. I had drifted to the surface of consciousness earlier, vaguely aware that Dia had slid from bed, perfect back and buttocks soon covered by robe, brown hair thrown back into place. And she had turned, smiling.

"Go back to sleep, darling. I'm going to make some tea. And a nice thick steak I bought for your noon feeding. I'll wake you when it's ready."

So I had let myself descend back into that gauzy netherworld of midday sleep, screened from the busy Cayman day by thick curtains and the generator whisper of air-conditioning.

And that's when I heard the *pop.* And then another. In my dreams, the beautiful Diacona Ebanks' hand dropped an egg. Or a lightbulb. And I was laughing at her. She was very lovely in the dreamy celestial light . . . and quite naked.

That's when the stifled scream told me it wasn't a dream.

I sat bolt upright in bed. The air conditioner filled the sudden quiet, along with the tick-tick-ticking of the alarm clock by the bed.

"Dia? Dia!"

She came walking mechanically through the bedroom door. There was a bewildered look on her perfect face. She wore the same burnt-orange robe. She had piled her hair atop her head after showering. Her right hand was clapped to her left breast as if saying the pledge of allegiance. She held her left arm out, reaching for me.

"Dia—what is it!"

She took two more zombielike steps, stumbled, then fell heavily on the floor. That's when I noticed the little rivulet of crimson streaming from her. She was straining desperately to hold it in, as if it were a leak that had to be plugged.

I was on my feet and beside her. Her eyes were distant, glazed.

"Dia, who did it? Who?"

Her left hand reached out and touched my face gently. Some grave understanding seemed to come into her eyes; then a stranger, unexpected expression—amusement.

"Dusky . . ." she whispered, the voice of a little girl.

And then she disappeared. . . .

In that curious vacancy of time and understanding which accompanies severe shock, the ambulance arrived and then the police. And the huge Irishman was not far behind.

I couldn't remember telephoning for help, but I did. And I couldn't remember ripping the door half off its hinges, running to the parking lot in search of the murderer, but it had to be me. I sat in a daze after they carted her away, half listening to the police captain tell me how it had probably happened.

"She was shot at very close range, sir. By a small-caliber weapon. Probably a .22. Twice. Through the heart. We figure she opened the door with the chain still on. Whoever did it didn't hesitate. You say you didn't hear anything until the gunshots?"

"No. I was asleep."

The police lieutenant was a somber black man in the crisp uniform the British assign to their tropical officers. He scribbled dutifully in his notebook. He didn't like asking the questions any more than I liked answering them.

"Did she say anything, sir, before she . . . passed away?"

"No. Just my name. Nothing else."

"Any idea who might have done it, sir?"

I started to tell him the truth, then stopped. Sure, I had an idea. Maybe more than just an idea. We had already told the cops to tail Sir Conan. And if they couldn't put two and two together, why make it easy for them?

That would just give me more time. More time to track him down on my own. In my mind's eye, I could see very clearly how I would take him; how I would force a confession and then tear his life away with my hands. I could see the handsome, slightly cruel English face of Sir Conan James; could see the way his dark eyes would look when I made him beg. . . .

"Is something wrong, sir? Shall I call a physician?"

The Cayman police lieutenant was looking at me strangely, reading the expression on my face.

"What? No. I'm fine. You were asking . . ."

"I was asking if you had any idea who might have shot Miss Ebanks."

"No. No idea. I just arrived on the island a few days ago."

"Did you come here on business?"

"He's workin' fer us, Lieutenant Campbell!" The big Irishman rambled across the expanse of apartment, hands in cutoff shorts, burly chest and shoulders straining against the white worsted shirt he wore. His red hair was mussed, as if he had come straight from bed.

"Commander O'Davis—this gentleman is working for you?"

"Aye. And if ye've asked all yer questions, Lieutenant, I'll be takin' him along now."

"Certainly, Commander."

The Irishman took me by the arm and led me outside. The police investigators were just finishing up, done with their measuring and powdering and outlining. Once more, a woman's life had ended with her form etched in chalk. Cynthia Rothchild. And now Diacona Ebanks. The first had been grim enough. The second I could not bear to see.

"You okay, Yank?" the Irishman said softly as he walked me down the stairs.

"Me? Sure. Everything's jake." My voice sounded odd, like the voice of some stranger on the edge of hysterics.

"Easy, lad, easy."

I squeezed into the Fiat and slammed the door. Outside the Sea Mist Apartments was a crowd of people, mostly islanders, many of them sobbing openly.

"The murder of an Ebanks is not taken calmly on Grand Cayman," O'Davis said as we backed onto the main road. "That poor lass of yours was probably related one way or another ta half the island population. They'll not let the judge go easy on 'im if they find out who done it—if they let 'im get to the judge, that is."

"*If* they find out who did it. You know damn well who killed her—the same maniac who killed Cynthia."

"Did ya tell the police that?"

I caught the Irishman's eyes. It was like looking into a mirror. His pale eyes were cold, frozen, bitter.

"Guess it slipped my mind."

"Good," he said. "That's me boy. Spoke with that fool Henderson at Government House this morning. That was before I got word about yer girl. He said the police sent a unit to Sir Conan's estate this mornin'. No one was there. Just the servants. Patrol cars are keepin' an eye open fer his car."

"Anymore word from the kidnappers?"

The Irishman shook his head. "They've got

full watches monitoring the VHF. But so far—
nothin'. I'm supposed ta ring in every half hour,
jest in case."

"They get anything out of the two Jamaicans?"

"At first the brutes wouldn't even admit ta
bein' part of a heroin ring. Finally gave in when
the evidence was presented—that an' the fact they
threatened them with murder charges fer the two
American drug runners. Had a real slick organi-
zation, they did. On the Jamaica end, their boss-
man would make contact with international
high rollers interested in makin' a quick killin'
on a drug deal. They'd meet the high rollers
here in Grand Cayman with the promise they'd
made arrangements ta buy X amount of heroin.
The high rollers were to finance the buy, then
take a major percentage of the sale but it never
worked that way, o' course. Jamaicans were
workin' both ends. Once they delivered the
money, the high rollers would just disappear—
or be scared inta never sayin' a word. After all,
no police force in the world would listen to their
tale o' woe about bein' flimflammed in a drug
deal. And the Jamaicans had no problem laun-
derin' the money through Grand Cayman with
all the international bankin' available." O'Davis
snorted. "Pretty damn smart, really. Said they
had a mandate from God. Needed the money
so the Rastafarians could take their prophesied

place as rulers of the world." The Irishman gave me a quick look. "Seem like there's more an' more loony-birds runnin' around lately?"

"Maybe. Or maybe they just get better press. A maniac has no more willing PR agent than your average reporter. One thing I do know— this island is going to have one fewer lunatic before I leave."

"Aye. I kin see that, brother MacMorgan. I kin see. But we still have the lost lad ta think about, don't forget."

"I haven't forgotten. I keep thinking kidnapping would fit right in with that Rastafarian mandate from God."

"The police are goin' over the trawler and the Canadian's home with a fine-tooth comb. If there's any sign of the boy, they'll find it. The Cayman regulars are all fine, studious lads. Not much crime here, so they do na get much chance ta use it. But that'll jest make 'em that much more determined ta succeed."

The gates at the Sir Conan James estate were open, so we just drove on in. A vintage battleship-gray Bentley was sitting inside the carport, garage door open. O'Davis identified it as Lady James' car. But there was no sign of Sir Conan James' Mercedes.

We decided to go in anyway. On the way, I

told Westy about my earlier encounter with the drunken succubus, Lady James. He clicked his tongue knowingly and said nothing.

"So I think it might be better if I talked to her by myself," I added. "There are still some things about the boy's room that bother me. The telescope was one thing—and that still doesn't make sense. His alarm clock was another."

The Irishman suddenly looked interested. "How's that, Yank?"

"Lady James said he usually got up about nine. But his alarm was set for five. I tried to tie it in with the telescope—maybe a meteor shower early in the morning. But there wasn't one. Nothing's adding up, Westy. And when your facts don't add up, it means you either don't have enough facts—or someone misled you."

"If yer tryin' ta get at somethin', Dusky, jest come right out and say it."

"Okay. I want you to do a little breaking and entering. While I'm talking to Lady James, I want you to go over this whole house. I'll keep her busy until you let me know you're done."

"But the police have already gone over the house."

"Yeah—looking for information. But not the boy."

"What?"

"Damn it, it's worth a try. This is a small island. They've had everyone but the Boy Scouts searching for him. They've done everything but go house to house—and that includes this house."

He shrugged. "It's true the two of 'em are crazy enough. But why would even Englishmen try somethin' so queer as ta . . ."

"I don't know. But it's worth a look."

I got out of the car feeling that odd floating sensation of sudden shock come over me. My footsteps on the drive echoed in my ear. Dia's dying eyes had seared themselves into my brain. . . . Work. That's what I needed now. I needed to bury myself in this mission; needed to forget everything else but the one lone goal; needed to blanket out the frozen specter of death, of dying men and screams in the night— everything but those eyes. Because I could never forget those dying eyes.

The same prim maid answered the door. She didn't even try to hide her disgust for me now. To her, I was just one more male dog, sniffing and pawing, anxious for another romp in bed with her hated mistress—and the lost boy be damned.

"Lady James is indisposed," she sniffed, blocking my entrance.

"I need to see her anyway." From the corner of my eye, I saw the Irishman cross the expanse of French windows, hunting for a back way in.

"She's not takin' visitors today!"

"It's about the boy."

For a moment, I thought she was going to break into grandmotherly tears. "Oh . . . have they found Master Thomas?"

"No. I'm sorry. But we're looking." She hesitated, and I added, "That's why I was here the other night, by the way. That and nothing else."

She inspected me momentarily like an old drill sergeant, then nodded her grudging approval. "She's seein' no one—like I said. But if it might help Master Tommy, then I won't say nothin' if you slip past me real quiet-like."

I went quickly up the carpeted staircase and found the door. I considered barging right in, then decided to keep the visit civil—at face value, anyway. So I knocked and opened the door.

She had just lit a cigarette. There was a fresh bottle of wine in the ice bucket. She wore striking white pleated pants and blouse, blond hair set in queenly ringlets. Had I not come to know the creature inside, she would have looked very beautiful indeed. I expected her to be outraged by my sudden entrance; instead she greeted me

with a theatrical delight—belied by the coldness
of her eyes.

"Well, how nice! My favorite eunuch is just
in time to join me for a glass of wine." She exhaled a slow cloud of cigarette smoke, then inhaled it abruptly through her thin nostrils.

"I'll just watch if you don't mind."

"Ah—how appropriate for someone with
your . . . sexual difficulties." She poured herself
a glass of wine, held it up in mock toast, drained
it and poured another.

"I'm looking for your husband."

"How nice."

"It's about your son."

Her eyes flared wide. "And just what in the
hell could you tell that bloody fool about my
son that you couldn't tell me?"

"Questions, that's all. I just want to ask him
some questions."

"Is that all you detective types do? Ask questions? I would have thought you would be out
looking."

"And I might say the same thing to you." I
meant it to hurt. And it did. I saw it in her eyes.
But she quickly lowered that British veil which
hides all and implies everything.

"Lately you seem to take especial delight in
hurting me, Mr. MacMorgan."

"An impersonal observer might call it an even exchange."

"I'm not that revolting, am I?"

"Don't underestimate yourself."

She crossed in front of me and took a seat on the divan, legs crossed, cigarette held erect. "You know, I didn't believe for a minute your story about being castrated in some horrible accident. I felt I owed it to my own self-esteem to play along with your little . . . fairy tale?" She smiled demurely. "Or is that a bad pun?" When I said nothing, she continued. "You forget that you were holding me very close. And you wanted me very much. That was . . . quite obvious."

"Do you know where your husband is or don't you?"

"I imagine he's out seducing some island whore. That's a normal course of recreation for him." She sipped at the wine, smiling. But the smile soon left her face. She tried to cover her sudden fear with flippancy. "For an awful moment, dear eunuch, I got the distinct impression you were about to hit me. But a big strong male like yourself wouldn't hit a woman—and a woman with a title at that."

"You don't care a goddamn for that boy, do you? Neither one of you airy, self-important bastards cares one ounce what's happening to him."

"Don't you say that! Don't you dare say that!" The change that came over her was explosive, unexpected. Wineglass crashing to the floor, she jumped to her feet and came stalking toward me. "You have no right to assume anything about my son! You have no right!" She exhaled a long breath, eyes wild, fighting for composure. When she was under better control, she stretched herself as if under some great weight. "You have no idea . . . no idea what I've been through," she said in a small voice. "I would do anything for Tommy."

"In that case, tell me where your husband is."

"I don't know!"

"He wasn't here at all last night?"

"No. I haven't seen him since the lawn party."

"Is that unusual?"

"Hardly. He's quite the roamer. Like a cat. The only thing he worries about is his women and the precious honor of the family name."

"He's got a weird way of showing it."

"And what's that supposed to mean?"

I watched her closely as I said it. "It means I think your wandering husband has gone even crazier than you know. I think he's developed a taste for murdering the women who turn him away. You might keep it in mind—if he cares enough about you anymore to ask."

"You're being ridiculous!"

"Am I?"

"Jimmy's a lot of things—a lot of very bad things. But he's no killer. I daresay he may have even spent a few hours out of the last night looking for Tommy."

"Why the change of heart?"

She paused long enough to light another cigarette. "There's no change of heart, MacMorgan. I hate him. I hate him quite thoroughly. I just don't think he's a murderer, that's all. I would have divorced him long ago if he . . . had not given me certain social freedoms and all the money I could want."

"You're the one who said he was brutal; that he liked to hurt his women."

She massaged her forehead with her fingers, thinking. Almost as if talking to herself, she said, "That's true. It's all true." She looked up at me, as if she had finally accepted the possibility. "My God, you don't really think he had something to do with those awful murders, do you?"

Behind me, I heard the Irishman's heavy footsteps on the stairs. I had heard him earlier—the sound of a door creaking. But this was his way of letting me know he was ready. I looked at the beautiful Lady James, the horror in her eyes. "Maybe," I said. "Just maybe. . . ."

17

At ten-fifteen that evening the phone rang. I could hear the Irishman's fluted voice coming from the cottage. He was a bulky silhouette against the window, nodding somberly.

For the hundredth time, I forced myself to piece together every chunk of random information I had acquired. I sat in the sand, arms bunched around knees, looking toward the starswept sea. Behind me, coconut palms framing the cottage rustled in the land breeze. And above, Orion the Hunter trailed its way across the chaotic rush of universe. Another beautiful night in the tropics. Only I saw it as anything but beautiful. Even the moon seemed laden with a red corona. And the freshening wind seemed to whisper of death.

The sea moved over the reef in gleaming swells.

My eyes moved upon the line of swells, focused, blurring, then focusing again. For how many centuries has man been burdening the sea with anthropomorphisms, assigning it human frailties? An angry sea, a nervous sea, a sea that brings peace—the words of men who do not know the sea. There is only the equation of salt and mineral and protoplasm; a perfect biological order subject to the whim of wind and universe, hell-bent on reproduction; a continuance. And what greater affirmation of life could someone want?

Thoughts drifted randomly as my mind cast back and forth seeking motive, method, and reason for the insanity of the last few days.

There had to be something I was missing; something I had overlooked.

But what?

What?

The Irishman's search had turned up negative. He had searched every room and closet in the house except for the kitchen, where the maid had busied herself washing dishes. But he had found no sign of young Thomas James. In the boy's room, he had confirmed my observation of the alarm clock. He had searched the stacks of rock albums, found the hidden magazines, and had proved to himself that the telescope had remained untouched since our earlier visit.

In short, he had found nothing new. So it had

to be me. I had to be overlooking something; some piece in the puzzle.

I heard O'Davis hang up the phone and clump across the porch outside.

"That was Government House, Yank."

I looked up. "They hear anything?"

"The kidnappers made contact twenty minutes ago by VHF. Same garbled voice. No recordin' of the lad this time. They want a plane ta drop the money about sixty miles north of here—not far from Cuban waters. He gave loran coordinates."

"Midnight tomorrow?"

"Aye."

O'Davis sat down beside me in the sand. "I figure you an' me can drop in place of the money. Maybe rig a big chute so we kin lash 'erselves together or somethin'. If the kidnappers stick to their word, the boy'll be safely away in a dinghy."

"Why not be waiting there with patrol boats and blast them out of the water?"

"They won't be comin' after the money with other boats or planes in the area—radar will probably tell 'em. An' they won't radio the lad's location till they're safely away. We're jest goin' ta have to chance takin' 'em by surprise, you and me. If we kin overpower 'em . . . make one of 'em talk . . . hell, who knows." The Irishman sighed. "This is bloody bad business, Yank. Nothin's workin' out. Everywhere ya look, nothin' but false trails. Sorry I brung ya in on it."

"Seems I remember getting you into a jam or two."

"Aye. But ya never got one of me ladies killed in the process."

And that's when it hit me. That's when one of the stray bits of information—an offhand remark—fell suddenly, neatly into place.

The Irishman looked at me. "What 'n hell's come over you? Look like ya've seen a ghost or somethin'."

"Maybe I have." I checked my watch. "You think that clunker car of yours can make one more trip into Georgetown?"

"Me fine little red Bess?" He snorted. "She'd take us ta Florida if they'd build a bloody bridge!"

"Good." I stood up, brushing off sand. "And let's take the Thompsons—just in case."

The gates to Sir Conan's estate were closed now. It bothered me. Maybe she had already gone and returned. We drove past once, straining to see house lights through the foliage.

"Looks like someone's still up."

"Aye. Maybe that ugly maid of theirs."

"We need to pull off the road—someplace we can watch the drive without being seen."

O'Davis found a wagon trail into the thicket of buttonwood and mangrove. He backed in and switched off the lights. Water in the Fiat's radiator gurgled. With windows open in the humid March night, mosquitoes soon found us, whining around our ears. I checked the green glow of Rolex. Ten forty-five.

"It has to be her," I said again with finality.

"It made sense when ya told me the first time, Yank. But the more I think about it, the crazier it sounds."

"It is. Because she's crazy. When she told me Sir Conan was the sadist it was some kind of weird personality transference. She's the one. I didn't catch it at first. And then it all fell into place. She said there was no way her husband could have committed both murders. And that was only an hour or so after Dia was killed. How could she have known?"

"Maybe Sir James came home and left again before we got there. She coulda been coverin' fer him."

"No way. She hates him. That's no act. And it's turned into a sexual quirk. But she's smart. She didn't want me to convince her too easily that her husband was the killer. But she's the one who planted the seed—remember? I can only guess about the kidnapping. But of one thing I'm sure: It was staged. You're the one who said it—just too many false trails. That boy is somewhere on this island. And I'm sure the woman knows where. Maybe Sir Conan, too. He's not stupid. When she snaked the kid away, he probably caught on quick. A staged kidnapping would be one way to divert attention from the fact your wife has committed murder and stolen your son."

"Family honor," the Irishman said softly.

"Right. As you said, he's got a lot of important connections and a lot of power. If the fictitious kidnappers never show, and they just happen to find the boy wandering around Grand Cayman, who's going to press for an investigation? I'm sure he'd pack the two of them up and be back in England before the dust even settled. He'd get some discreet psychiatric hearing held for his crazy wife, send the boy away to some private school. When you think about it, what alternative does he have? Tell the court his wife has a nasty habit of killing his mistresses, both real and suspected? That's like admitting your wife wants a divorce because you only beat her occasionally."

"Okay, Yank. Say she killed me little Cynthia because she suspected her of havin' a fling with

Sir James. An' maybe she got ta worryin' about me havin' seen the whole thing from the bushes and decided ta do away with me, too. That still doesn't explain how she got ahold of Cynthia's Jaguar."

"No," I said, "it doesn't. We'll ask her about it when we see her."

We waited and waited in the darkness and mosquitoes, and still nothing happened.

The Irishman, face on huge hand, drifted off to sleep, snoring softly. I sipped at a third bottle of Red Stripe from the little plastic cooler in the back, spitting Copenhagen out the window.

And then I saw it: a sudden splash of light on the trees along the driveway.

I nudged O'Davis. He came awake gaping and stretching. He grabbed my bottle of beer, chugged it halfway down, and shook himself. "There, and I'm feelin' much better. What's afoot?"

"A car, I think. Coming down the drive."

The lights continued to pan along the high copse at the edge of the yard, then switched off abruptly. It was nearly two A.M. and the moon was drifting low toward the westward horizon, but there was still enough sheen to see the dim shape of Lady James' Bentley. It stopped at the gate, a courtesy light flared on, and she got out,

looking each way down the road. Involuntarily,
I found myself ducking back. But the chances of
her seeing us were zero.

She pushed the high wrought-iron gate open,
returned to the car, and turned left toward
Georgetown, lights still off until she was well
down the road.

When O'Davis deemed it safe, we pulled out
and followed her in darkness, the winding asphalt a gray ribbon. Land crabs were dark
shapes, scurrying before us.

At the edge of Georgetown, when she disappeared around a curve, the Irishman switched
his lights on. It was a Sunday night and there
was no traffic. But the city was illuminated, silent. And a car with no lights would just arouse
suspicion—maybe Lady James'.

She headed out the Ocean Road along Seven
Mile Beach. The Bentley toured along at sixty,
and O'Davis had to make the Fiat kick and sputter to keep up. I noted wryly that once again
we seemed headed for the little settlement of
Hell. But at the convergence of roads, she veered
right instead of left.

It was a small beach house not far from the
Canadian's estate. We had driven the final two
miles in darkness, headlights off on the desolate
stretch of highway. The beach house showed itself in the distance as a stilted shape behind a

line of Australian pines at the edge of the sea.
We did not see Lady James turn in so much as
notice that her car just disappeared.

"That's got to be it," I said, whispering for no
good reason.

"We kin park in the trees and walk the, say,
last half mile?"

"Let's make it the last three-quarters of a mile,
just in case they have a guard posted."

The Irishman switched off the engine and let
his little red car coast down the road, finally
pulling off into a line of mangrove cover. I
grabbed the two Thompsons—freshly stripped
and oiled—and we headed along the gray strip
of highway in the silence of Grand Cayman,
two-thirty A.M. A night heron squawked somewhere, and our footsteps seemed unnaturally
loud upon the shell marl.

As we got closer, the beach house grew in
shape and definition. It was a stylish board-and-
batten cottage built on rows of stilts. It glowed
pale white in the moonlight.

The covering of Australian pine needles blan-
keted our approach. We moved from shadow to
shadow, both at once, keeping a sharp eye out
for a guard.

But there was none.

The house was dark. But the Bentley sat in
the drive—along with Sir Conan's Mercedes. I

couldn't figure it out. But then the Irishman nudged me, pointing. Like many stilthouses, this one had a small paneled apartment built beneath. A yellow rind of light filtered from beneath the door.

"May be a window on the other side."

"Aye. Let's have a look."

We moved along the seaward side of the house. The surf roared and spouted upon the bluff below. The wind was heavy, weighted with salt.

We could hear the voices even before we got to the window; animated voices in half-whisper. I lifted one eye up over the windowsill, the Irishman looking from the other side. There was a kerosene lamp on one of those plank picnic tables stained to resemble redwood. Near the lamp was a jar of peanut butter, half a loaf of bread, and a dozen tins of canned food.

Sir Conan James and his alcoholic wife stood face to face in the haloing light. She looked angry. He just looked worried . . . and very, very tired.

". . . because I'm not about to let you back out now, that's why!" she was yelling in the same hoarse whisper. She stabbed out her cigarette in an empty can and lit another.

"But Elizabeth, can't you see, it's hopeless! I was mad to go along with it in the first place!"

He took her pleadingly by the shoulders. "Can't you understand? Murder has been committed! Not one. Two! And the blood is on your hands, my dear, *your hands!*"

She knocked his arms away. "Don't expect me to cry over your two dead whores. I won't, do you hear me? I won't! I warn you, Jimmy, if you give in now I'll tell them it was you who killed them. And just see what kind of scandal that brings. Why, the American is already sure that it was you!" Her eyes narrowed and her voice dropped. "Don't you see, it *will* work. Tomorrow night when the whole Cayman police force is off looking for Tommy, a chartered plane will be waiting for us at the airport. We'll fly to Kingston. People can be bought there. We'll have our papers changed; well go to South America. It would take them years to get us out of there—if they tried. But they won't. Your friends will see to that."

"And give Tommy just one more reason to hate us." Conan James wiped a weary hand across his face, near tears it seemed. "Elizabeth, please stop fighting the inevitable. We've already been much too bad to have a son so smart. My women, your men, my drug dealings—he knew about them all along. Last night when they killed Cribbs and the others, we could hear the shooting. He thought it all very funny!"

For the first time, Lady James seemed to waver. Her eyes clouded and her lower lip trembled. Sir Conan went on, "Elizabeth, tomorrow morning I'm going to the authorities and tell them everything. It'll be hard on all of us, but no one will be hanged—of that I am sure." His voice faltered, cracking. "I've been a bad husband, Elizabeth. And a worse father. But it's not too late for us. Please believe me. It's not too late!"

The regal veneer of the woman, all the hatred and bitterness, melted into one long anguished sob. She fell forward into Sir Conan James' arms. "Oh, Jimmy, do you really think so? If it could only be true . . . I'd do anything. *Anything.* You're all I've ever wanted . . . you and Tommy." She looked up at him, tears streaming from her eyes. "I feel so lost, Jimmy . . . so lost and helpless. The drugs and the stolen car, and now this. Please tell me you're right . . . that there is hope!"

For the first time, I noticed something moving in the corner; something unseen in the darkness. He came crawling into the small corona of lamplight, heels pulling, hips hunching like a worm. His feet were tied, hands bound behind him. I remembered the picture I had seen in his room: the huge brown eyes, the perfect translucent skin. Young Thomas James was a little taller than I had expected, but the features still suggested frailty, vulnerability, and that curious sensitivity of the super-intelligent. His head had been shaved. It prodded at some memory . . . the rock albums I had seen in his room. Punk rock. The skinheads. Picture of a bald rock warrior holding a rifle.

His lips pouted like a child. "Don't believe him, Mummy," he said in a small, firm voice. "Please don't believe him. He's quite mad, you know."

Lady James' arms slid away from her husband. Her expression was a mixture of love and horror. She reached out with a pale hand, touching her son's face. He leaned toward her for a moment, then his head swung around and his teeth snapped, gnashing like an attack dog's, just missing her arm. His eyes were murderous; dark orbs of madness.

"And what if he escapes again?" said Sir Conan, voice quaking, taking her in his arms. *"Just what do we do if he escapes again?"*

I backed away from the window, touching my finger to my lips. We stopped only once: to inspect a car hidden beneath trees and a layer of tarp. The Jaguar.

All the way to East End, neither of us spoke a word. . . .

18

Twenty-one days after Diacona Ebanks' funeral, I sat in the fresh sunlight of a Key West April wondering just what in the hell was taking him so long.

I sat aboard my thirty-four-foot custom-built sportfisherman, *Sniper*, drinking a cold beer and watching the late-season tourists gawk at the fish gurry in the trash cans. There was one guy I really liked: a fiftyish Ohio-type in white socks, sandals, Bermuda shorts, Hawaiian shirt, and a hat with Budweiser cans sewn to it. He had to have style to throw himself so totally upon the mercy of a cliché. The guy grinned at me and waved. I waved back.

I checked my watch for the umpteenth time, then went to get another beer.

My last days on Grand Cayman had not been easy. I'd felt gauzy, out of sorts, out of touch. Nothing seemed real. And I couldn't seem to arouse even the energy to question my lethargy. Sooner or later, the crazies catch up with you. They pry at the brain and deflate the heart.

And the Irishman had been no better. But he, at least, could bury himself in his reports to Government House. The international press got hold of the story, of course. The newspapers feed on the blood and misery of others.

Yet the newspapers didn't piece together all the story. They rarely do. Even Westy and I had to drop it all with a few questions unanswered. The kid's alarm clock had been my first tip-off that it might be something other than an ordinary kidnapping—if there's such a thing as an ordinary kidnapping. He usually got up at nine—so why, on the day of his disappearance, did he rise before the sun? Because his mother had somehow discovered he had killed Cynthia Rothchild, and she had cooked up a scheme to free her precious child of the responsibility. Even that late in the game, the kid had to be hanging on to some thread of reality. Because he went along with it. And he still seemed sane enough for his mother to trust him alone in the beach house—thus the telescope, so that he could signal her at night if he needed something. A phone call was out of the question. The Cayman police had the wire tapped.

But the brilliant, demented Thomas James didn't cling to rational thought for long. He had tried to kill me—thinking it was Westy—out of some misplaced jealousy. And then he had gone after my poor, lost Diacona. His last reasonable act had probably been allowing his mother to tape his bogus plea for cooperation with the kidnappers. The noble Sir Conan James, heavily in debt—as the news stories did reveal—and struggling to recoup his once great fortune through drug running, had little choice but to go along with it. He was terrified of scandal . . . and he had no idea how bad it was going to be.

Even so, Sir Conan and Lady James had handled it all with admirable British stoicism. Even grace. Poor, demented Tommy had been arrested immediately and sent to a special sanatorium in the Swiss Alps, leaving his parents to deal with their own arrest charges. But in every newspaper photo I saw they were clinging to each other, hand in hand, giving the reporters the same simple monotone statement: "At only fourteen years old, the doctors insist there's hope."

Of course that didn't bring my Dia back. Or Westy's Cynthia. But sometimes, when the world turns gray and moody, and the wind bespeaks madness, you grab at any particle of justice you can find.

As the man says: Something's better than nothing at all.

So in the depths of my depression, the Irishman had tried to brace me with the promise of a trip. A boat trip with Penn International Gold reels instead of Thompson submachine guns. And beer. Lots of cold beer. And rather than let him know his ploy was a miserable failure, I agreed. But then the idea began to grow on me. Why not bake the memories away with sun and good fish and unknown islands shimmering on the turquoise curve of horizon?

So now I was waiting. And he was late. As usual.

I cracked another frozen Tuborg, cut the foam with my tongue, and went back to the aft deck, taking my seat in the fighting chair. And that's when I saw him coming: a huge red-haired gnome, seabag over his shoulder, knees pointed out awkwardly as he pedaled along the Garrison Bight sidewalk on my old ten-speed bike.

When he saw me, he made an awful face. "Yank, I thought ya said ye'd have transportation waitin' fer me at the airport?" he yelled.

"I said you'd have wheels," I yelled back. "I just didn't say how many."

He leaned the bike against a palm, dumped his seabag, and jammed his fists on his hips, smiling all the while. "It's a bloody bi-cycle!"

"Can't slip anything past you, O'Davis. Besides, I don't own a car."

His face mimicked outrage. "Ya don't own a—and ya had the gall ta mean-mouth me sweet little Italian Bess! Didn't even meet me at the airport ta boot!"

"We'd've looked pretty silly riding one bike. Besides, fat as you are, you can use the exercise." I winked at him. "But look on the bright side, O'Davis. With you being late and all, I went ahead and bought all the supplies—not that I ever hoped to see any money from you. I got ten cases of Tuborg and ten cases of that crap you drink—stout. And enough food to feed a haybalers' convention. That ought to last a few weeks."

He snorted. "Few days is more like it. Only ten cases of stout?"

"It'll get you away from the world for a while."

"Aye, an' we're both more'n deservin', I'm thinkin'." He swung the seabag over his shoulder and eyed me shrewdly. "It's a crazy line 'a work we've chosen fer ourselves, Brother Mac-Morgan."

"You sound like a man who might want out."

"Might? *Might?* I've been doin' a lot of thinkin', Yank, an' there's no might or mebee about it. I do want out. I'm tired of the killin' and the nighttime cops 'n robbers while our chubby bureaucrat bosses sit in their sweet offices and get rich with our blood."

I stepped from the dock aboard *Sniper*. She felt fresh and sure, ready for sea. Maybe O'Davis was right. Maybe I was ready, too. After all, wasn't it just a game? One vast and meaningless blood sport that encouraged the chaos it supposedly fought? It was no revelation—maybe because O'Davis was only verbalizing what I had been feeling all along.

"That story I told Diacona—the one about me starting a charter service on Grand Cayman? Could be it's not such a bad idea after all?"

The Irishman gave me a broad smile. "Now yer talkin', Yank. Too many pretty tourist ladies fer me ta' handle on my own! An' I think ya might even make some money!"

"Then for the winter I could come back here to Key West and guide—I wouldn't want to give up fishing."

"Fishin', is it? Odd ya should mention that. I've been thinkin' about doin' some charterin' of me own. Right here in Key West of all places!"

I chuckled and shook my head. I stood face to face with the Irishman, the beard on his big jaw rust-colored in the spring sunlight. His pale eyes actually seemed merry, without a care, for the first time since I had met him one morning in Mariel Harbor, Cuba.

"You're serious, aren't you?"

He took a huge breath of sweet morning air, then spit in the palm of his hand and held it before me.

"Ah, I am . . . I am. Shake on it, lad, an' we'll tell them all ta go ta hell in a dogcart."

I expected myself to hesitate. But I didn't. His handshake was as strong and sure as my own. . . .